Caldera: Notes from the Pit
Venting A Sarcastic Soul

Edward Fuller

CALDERA: NOTES FROM THE PIT

VENTING A SARCASTIC SOUL

EDWARD FULLER

PUBLISHED BY FASTPENCIL

Copyright © 2014, 2016 Edward Fuller

ISBN 978-1-68348-463-9 (pbk)
ISBN 978-1-68348-464-6 (digital)

Printed in the United States of America.

For Bev

Thank you to friends and family, past and present, known and unknown.

ൟ

Acknowledgments

Life is a harsh teacher, but I will not leave her alone.

CONTENTS

1

WESTBOUND

Never say never,
what you will or won't do,
leave yourself leeway,
in case you have to,
pride is not possible,
when you find yourself thus,
cramped, tired, and aching,
on a westbound bus,
gazing out the window,
legs eased into the aisle,
try to see something,
it's gonna be a while,
arrogance snuffed,
not qualified to matter,

and the bus goes 'round,
with our social strata,
some workers, soldiers,
and even the insane,
families and some folks,
just looking to start again,
all ages aboard,
a lonely seething mass,
comforting themselves thinking,
" ... and this too, shall pass,
This lifeblood is pulsing,
from American shore to shore,
Liberty said it best:
"Give me your tired——your poor ... "
Who can know hearts,
beating within "huddled masses,"
All hungry for something,
better have your bus passes ...

2

BARE ESSENTIALS

Death comes to us in many ways. For some it comes with glory. For others it is a prolonged visitor that keeps them hanging onto life until they welcome its final company. Most of the time Death is unwelcome and inglorious. Complete randomness makes Death's job easier. It can fall upon whoever it chooses whenever it pleases.

"This is some bullshit! Not like this." Beau thought.

So many missteps flashed before his eyes that he had trouble keeping focused on a survival strategy. Faces he held dear and long-forgotten ones flashed before his eyes. He thought of his mother. He thought of his wife and kids.

Beau was standing atop a toilet seat in a traveler's rest area on I-85 South in Brunswick County, Virginia. He held a 4-inch bladed pocketknife at the ready in his right hand. He knew it was not going to help him much if a confrontation was coming up. He supported his six foot 300 pound frame with his left hand. It was tingling from loss of circulation as he braced himself against the metal bathroom stall door. He hoped the little circular lock would hold. He tried to remain still and quiet.

The automatic toilet flushed.

"Why did I have to stop here of all places?" he thought frantically, preparing for the fight of his life.

It had all been going according to plan. The Alberta Rest Area was the midpoint on his midnight run from Philly, PA to Charlotte, NC. It was the logical choice. He had been tired and had caught himself nodding off behind the wheel of his tractor-trailer. He had started seeing things on the road that weren't there which meant he was almost in dream-state. Plus he had needed to use the bathroom.

The Welcome Center was well-lit and newly built. The low elongated red-brick structure was clean and the yellowing grass had received its final cutting for the fall. Pine needles littered the ground along with acorns and shriveled brown oak leaves. The season's first numbing breaths of frosty wind rustled through the late fall night.

Tall almost leafless oaks and dark pine trees stood like haggard sentries by the sides and behind the building. They had stripped themselves down to the bare essentials needed to survive the coming winter. The sky was aglow with twinkling stars the way it is when you go far beyond city limits.

All had been quiet leaving him to his thoughts. Beau wondered how he had ended up in a job he hated so much. He knew. He had forgot to live within his means. He had over-reached the bare essentials, and now found himself a slave to possessions that he rarely saw anymore. He was losing his friends and family. He had always been a great acquaintance but was now an absent father and friend. No depth except for debts.

Those were his relationships now. He had thought they mattered. Now faced with death, they were the farthest thing from his mind. His mind was a torture chamber in which he dwelled alone berating himself.

He had muttered "Can't keep nothing nice…" when he had seen the overturned trash can and litter strewn in front of the glass-paned atrium of the rest area facility.

"Oh, are people too lazy to open doors for themselves now?" he had grumbled as the sliding glass doors slid open at his approach to the entrance.

"I'll be seeing you later. I promise." he said to the well-stocked snack and drink machines because he had no one to talk to. The glaring flourescent lighting inside the place made him feel like being silly because it improved his morose mood.

Beau had rounded a curved wall and entered the men's restroom. After closing the door to his stall he saw that vandals had already begun tagging the stall door with graffitti.

"I guess that's why they don't put doors on these bathrooms anymore. They'll just mess it up."

He was preparing to exit the stall when he had heard the outside automatic doors whisk open.

CRASH! The sound of breaking glass resounded in the lobby and echoed in the bathroom. This was followed by muffled heavy footsteps and weird unidentifiable noises.

"Whoa...what the hell?" he thought and delayed his exit listening.

"Probably the same idiot who dumped the trash busting into the snack machine."

Beau stepped atop the toilet seat in case someone looked in.

Beau's pulse quickened as he heard scratching sounds and wrappers being ripped open. The sound of scores of pieces of hard candy hitting the ceramic floors. Snuffling. Snorting. Licking. Chewing. Smacking lips. Gutteral breaths. Then, the toilet had automatically flushed. The noises had ceased. Then, heavy padding footsteps had approached and stopped outside his stall.

"Man, if only it was a normal damned toilet."

A black furry snout poked under the door and snuffled once more curiously.

Mama Bear was pregnant. She was readying herself for her winter's nap. She needed 20,000 calories a day to prepare herself. She had been subsisting on the bare essentials but they had become sparse. The trash had been a great supplement to the nuts and berrries that were disappearing. The snack machines had been even better. She was sure that she would rest soundly after her final discovery of a more filling and substantial meal in the rest area bathroom.

Dearly beloved, we are gathered here today to bury a guy who had forsaken taking care of the bare essentials and himself became the bear essentials.

3

BIBLE BELT BABBLE

"This is going 2 hurt me more than it hurts
U..."

My Stepdaddy,
Was a spiritual man,
The Bible in his heart,
And a belt in his hand,
Kept his head down at work,
But his eyes toward God,
He spoiled not the child,
And spared not the rod,
A scripture for the crime,
of punishment dealt,
Was read piously,

Before the raising of welts,
Tightly gripping the wrists,
A swift quiver of wind,
Stinging culminations,
The strap struck the skin,
Helpless in rage,
Brace for the next blow,
Inner focus to try,
Not to let hurt show,
When he had tired,
And panting watched me cry,
I would run to my room,
Until tears ran dry,
He may have meant well,
But violence was taught,
The lesson I chose,
Was not to get caught,
Beatings forged my exterior,
To mask pain I feel,
And never let authority,
Put a crack in my will,
An unlimited dynamo,
From which I can draw,
Bolts of wrath with little,
Provocation at all,

I learned to calculate,
When to strike,
When to wait,
Calm facade harboring,
The stormiest inner states,
A diplomatic demeanor,
A warrior beneath,
Pleasant smile on my face,
As I grind my teeth....

4

REFLECTION ON A SHOESHINE GUY

West Texas was scorching,

Even the breeze was hot,
A traveler trudged weary,
Into an El Paso truckstop,
Faded jeans frayed at hem,
Shower stuff in his duffle,
Wrinkled tee, dusty boots,
In - he - shuffled,
He saw an old Shoeshiner,
The color of brown leather,
Sinewed, tall, sere,
Made by time and weather,
Their eyes met briefly,

Maybe a glint of pity,
He hadn't seen brothers,
Shining shoes in his city,
"What a slave mentality."
He thought with disgust,
"Where's his ambition?"
he wondered covered in dust,
He ate, drank, showered,
Then sauntered back by,
It was then he first saw,
The gleam those eyes,
The old one acknowledged him,
With a hop in his step,
Brush, polish, buff,
Was the rhythm he kept,
He bounced to his work,
And had customers in line,
Headphones kicking jazz,
He worked keeping in time,
Quick with a smile,
A showman with skills,
Upbeat in manner,
Just oozing goodwill,
The traveler was leaving,
And was met with a grin,

Then a look of horror…
"Say man, ARE THOSE TIMBS?"
"Yep—uhh—yeah—umm—
What you want and why?"
"This ones's ON ME…"
Was the Shineman's reply,
"Good Lord—boy,"
The elder near hollered,
"Don't these cost more,
Than a hundred dollars!?"
He brushed then wiped them,
On his pace again,
Lit them aflame,
Burnt off scuffs rough ends,
The offender was nervous,
But flame was soon snuffed,
The boots were wiped clean,
Then polished, then buffed,
O how uncomfortable was that exalted seat,
The traveler thought of Jesus,
Washing his disciples' feet,
He tried no longer to,
Stereo-typify,
But take pride in his work,
Like the Shoeshine Guy.

5

Stuck on Simmer

I NEVER have been one,
Who could easily turn the page,
Brother was the good son,
I was one dark with rage,
While he brushed off insults,
Revenge I always vowed,
I am NOT talking to myself!
I'm simply THINKING OUT LOUD!
Why can't I brush off slights?
Whether real or just perceived,
Grudges weigh heavily as burdens,
Forgiveness WOULD bring relief,
Now THERE'S a concept...

That should have been ingrained,
My parents really tried,
I was Bibically trained,
But was particularly drawn,
To the great warriors of God,
And stories of God's wrath ...
My parents spared not the rod,
I was taught that the world,
Would be inherited by the meek,
But just got my ass kicked,
When I turned the other cheek,
So I became the little nerd,
Who would drop his books and fight,
Get a paddling at school,
And whipped with belts at night,
And for all the talk of mercy,
I remember very little shown,
Pissed at self and the world,
And now the cynic's grown,
Parents say: "You never went to jail."
As if I should applaud,
Actually discouraged college,
Waiting on the kingdom of God,
This world is ending soon,
They still say to this day,

Lord is coming as a thief,
With non-believers I could not play,
Reading, drawing, writing,
Don't require someone else,
Solitudes retreated to,
Went to movies by myself,
History, Arts, Science,
Knowledge became prodigious,
Then I felt cheated,
And not at all religious,
When you find your whole upbringing,
Was based on 2000 year old tales,
People rising from the dead,
man alive in Whale,
One can't help but get,
A wary distrust of authority,
Especially if like myself,
You're a minority of a minority.

6

TEXAS POPSICLE

Officer Schaeffer approached the frozen heap that lay in a fetal position amidst the low scraggled brush, cacti, and rocky dust at her feet. A tiny lizard deserted a sunny rock. It skittered over a reddish-brown glazed clenched fist, and darted into a root shaded-crevice.

It was late August just north of Laredo, Texas. The late morning was so hot that steam rose from the ground as welcome rain evaporated from the night before. Hannah observed that interstate I-35 was already dry as cars and 18-wheelers barreled past at highway speeds.

Invisible grit kept getting in her eyes with each passing gust. She tried to take in the whole scene and think objectively.

"This is odd. Makes no sense. I've seen plenty of these folks who died out here in the heat trying to sneak past the Border Patrol, but frozen is a first." she muttered almost herself, and wiped her brow.

"No shit? That dude is frozen? You kidding me lady? It's gotta be over 80 degrees out here already." Jesus asked while striding up to the body for a closer look.

Hannah couldn't help but smile at the F.N.G's enthusiasm. "See for yourself whippa-snappa." she said as she pointed at the thawing mass with a jaded curiosity.

"Oh it's whippa-snappa now huh? That's ok. Call me whateva. I'm gonna still be gettin' paid regardless of what you call me." Jesus Brown teased back. He was trying to get a good look at the frostbitten features of the deceased without messing up the scene for the forensic team that had already been notified.

Officer Schaeffer sucked her teeth, then exhaled and began exaggeratingly massaging her hands and wrists. "I come in to work traffic and now we got a homicide on our plate. I hope you don't have carpal tunnel. You type fast youngin?"

"Enough with all the damned youngins, whippa-snappas, and fucking new guys… yeah I know what F.N.G. means! Especially if you want access to these non-arthritic fingers to type OUR report lady." Jesus said with an exasperated look at his smirking matriarchal sensei. She batted her eyes at him sarcastically. "Why does she wear that light-blue eyeshadow?" he thought.

Then her eyebrows went up and apart as her eyes widened. Hannah chuckled and put a hand on her chest.

"I just had a thought how that guy got here. Lord have mercy on 'em, Haysoose." She looked ashamed and said, "I shouldna' been laughing."

Officer Brown looked at the short stocky woman like she was putting him on. He had been hazed quite a bit since finishing the police academy. Then a sly gleam came into his eye and he stepped away from the body towards her.

"Really? What you got under that little blond beehive of yours? We got us a frozen Mexican dude in Texas in the middle of August. If you think you know, AND you end up being right…You can call me youngin' and I will type up the report. If you wrong then you have to do the typing and buy me a shake. Deal?"

To his surprise, Hannah Schaeffer sidled up and firmly shook his hand. The old gal had a sure grip. "Carpal tunnel my ass." he murmured with a new sense of foreboding.

"A trucker called this in over the CB didn't he?" she asked Jesus as if trying to remember things more clearly.

"Yep. Said he saw what he thought was a coyote and some big birds picking at something not far off the road that looked like a curled up dead guy on the northbound side of I-35 near milemarker 15." Julio answered taking notes. "I was on my job and you were getting us coffee." he added with a snicker.

"Did he give you his name or truck number, company, or anything that we could get a holdt of 'em with?" Hannah asked as if she already expected a negative answer. She shaded her eyes that scanned theÂ side of the road headed north.

"Nah... come to think of it he was pretty exact about the location though." Officer Brown responded with a nice cold milkshake on his mind.

"Ain't it odd that no other trucks or cars saw nothin? I mean a coyote and a bunch of birds weren't here when we pulled the cruiser up. That ol' boy knew sumthin..." Hannah stated matter-of-factly, her doughy chin set firm.

"Don't tell me... but how? What could he have done? Killed the guy and froze him? He doesn't have any wounds except frostbite from what I can see."Officer Brown replied with some apprehension. His hope for a milkshake fading and the prospect of typing a lot of paperwork looming.

"My guess is he froze 'em and kilt him. Couldn't hear him over the sound of the truck. Probably by accident I reckon. Felt bad when he discovered him and called in where he dumped him." Hannah said looking stoicly at the northern horizon.

Jesus scratched at his pad then chewed his pen and frowned. "So you think he got stuck in a refrigerated trailer? Hmmmm…that explains the ice glaze. Yeah, I'm picking up what you are puttin' down…yeah. He's beating on the doors with his fists but those trailers lock from the outside. Helluva way to go."

"This little fella had made it across I guess, but needed a ride past the Border Patrol further north. Sometimes they check trailers but most times they don't. He hopped in this guy's trailer to stowaway north and to get out of the rain last night."

"Lordy. Go ahead and finish woman. You set me up for long day at the office. I might as well know. Wait. If the doors lock from the outside how did he close the door to the trailer?" Julio wanted to know.

"He probably had help. These folks ain't usually solo. If the truckdriver saw that his trailer door was open he would've busted the guy or asked him for money. If the door was closed and the driver had checked it and found it empty yesterday, he probably wouldn't have bothered. Got message for his next load and you know what happened next I figure..." Hannah said and eyed Jesus Brown expectantly.

"Dayuumm. He set his trailer temp to pre-cool down and started rolling to his load shipper. Judging by this dude I'd say -10 degrees. Yeeeshh! I hate to even think about it." Jesus answered with a shiver.

"I bet we can find out who did it young man."

"That'll take some doing won't it little lady?"

"Not much. All these trucks are tracked by satellite and most of these guys have cell phones. The record is out there. We're looking for a driver who got to his shipper...

probably a frozen meat packing place near here…left because he opened his trailer doors and found a body…got the hell outta there and dumped it here…then maybe went back south to get his load, still gotta pay the bills and freight is hard to come by…and only radioed it in as he was passing the scene northbound the second time because he felt bad. He wasn't trying to kill nobody. He was just negligent."

"I hate to say I think you are right Miss Hannah. How do you know so much and can't be bothered to type up this report?"

"Big Daddy Schaeffer is a trucker."

7

ROADSIDE CROSSES

Calculating, calculating…
My eyes move constantly,
I must read every sign,
I have five different mirrors to check,
Three blind spots to guard,
I must expect 4-wheelers to be impatient,
I must expect them to do the wrong thing,
I have 13 gears to shift through,
I ignore my cellphone,
I must block out homesickness,
Two foci:
Be ontime and dont hit or be hit,
Check the GPS,
Check the trip plan,

Are the routes suitable for 80 thousand
pound 18-wheelers?
Are the bridges and overpasses high enough
to pass through,
What mile marker am I at?
What speed am I averaging?
What is my estimated time of arrival?
What are my revenues, expenses, and profits?
Are my directions accurate?
Maintain a safe following distance,
Small corrections, control, be cool,
Do I have adequate air brake psi to stop this
thing?
What percentage slope is this mountain?
What does my dispatcher have in my satellite
link queue now?
Thinking. "Will D.O.T. inspect my rig
today?"
Where's the pileup?!
Get on the CB...rerouting...detour,
Timetable is fucked! Is this route restricted?
10-4.
SHIT!! Fatality...fatality...injury,
Wreckage...stop gawking people!

LETS GO DAMMIT!
Keep moving fuckers before somebody gets
hit in the ass!
No one will remember,
Once they get where they are going,
People risk their lives to save a few seconds of
travel time.
Nobody expects to die this day,
Thats why they are called accidents...
The mass rushes by,
Like water around a dead stone in a stream,
The only remembrance of these dead,
If so loved,
Are little roadside crosses,
In various states of decor or decay...
For a moment my calculations stop...
And I wonder what were their thoughts that
final day...
Cigarettes, diseases, guns, whatever...
Pale versus death by driving...
Love your selves more than that few seconds
you may save...
I am tired of you making me think of your
insignificant mortality...and mine.

8

THE ROLLOVER

The last thing I heard was a click-clack-click,
Pow! I blacked out and don't remember the
rest of it,
It started with my cuz saying:
"Let's hit this lick…"
"He ID'd you as the shooter."
"Ain't this some bullshit…"
"Now you can help yourself…"
"I bet he talked HIMSELF out of it…"
"This isn't about him.
This is about you."
"But he's the wannabe gangsta dealer!"
"We heard you packed the heat too."
"That lying ass punk…"

"We'll play you the witness's tape."
"Skip the WITNESS bullshit,
I know THAT nigga's dodging jail rape."
"What would make you say that?"
"He can't scrap a lick,
he's all talk, no heart,
and can't keep a woman with his dick."
"But YOU had his back,
that's what our sources SAID.
Tried to roll a customer,
and put a gun to his head."
"I didn't say I did it,
that night was a blur."
"There's brains and blood in the hallway,
where a tip said you were."
"I was drunk and don't remember."
"That's some defense,
the thing about this crime,
is that it makes no damn sense."
"I DIDN'T ROB NOBODY!"
"You left his money in his hand."
"That nigga flinched, the trigger clenched…"
"So you shot him and ran?"
"I just don't know…"

Eyes wet, jaw clenched.
Running to the trash can.
Vomiting, stomach wrenched.
"That's a lot to carry around.
A family man died last night.
You might not have meant to do it,
but we've got to make this right!"
"I'm sorry ... I'm sorry,
I don't even know,
but if I'm going to prison ...
MY COUSIN IS GONNA GO!"

9

B.S. TO S.O.S. (SOMEONE SPECIAL)

We can still be friends—right?
We can still be friends—right.
Let by-gones be bygones,
Like what happened last night,
Don't know how I got here,
Do know that I had beer,
A few bumps and tequila,
Somehow I got locked in here,
I know my knuckles bleeding,
But that could be misleading,
Policia said I struck a pimp,
That doesn't mean I'm cheating,
So now I am in prison,

Stop yelling girl just listen,
Oh yeah… I am in Mexico,
In jail with no conviction,
I could not help but think of you,
Or think of proper words to say,
You are my moment of clarity,
Thats why I'm calling you today,
All I needed was a quarter,
To get back across the border,
Got my pockets picked clean,
By a hooker/stripper's daughter,
No we didn't screw No!
I just watched her strip show,
No No don't hang up now!
I was drunk but I would know!
Oh my head is pounding,
And my heart burns with pain,
Please wire me some money,
Just so I can see you again,
Here I'm just a Gringo,
Despite the color of my skin,
And if you post my bail,
I'll never leave you again,
You think I'm just hungover,

But heartache is why I'm really sick,
Girl help me out to be with you,
I'm honest because you can handle it,
Thanks for accepting charges,
On my one collect call,
I just need you credit card number,
and your love and that is all….

10

DEATH OF A USED CAR SALESMAN (SHARK OUT OF WATER)

The life that I live,
Is not the life I sought,
I gaze at a focal point,
Looking for positive thoughts,
Why must I always leave,
The worn well-trodden path,
Get into a groove,
Then jump tracks to aftermath?
Why must I constantly move,
Am I a shark out of water?
Am I capable of love?

Little time for wife and daughters …
I'm breathing slowly,
Without my razor pearled grin,
Predatory with ambition,
Exterior that cuts the skin,
You will never see me coming,
The mechanism well greased,
I'll find common ground,
And put you at your ease,
Do I have your attention?
Great, take action follow me,
Do I have what you want?
My observation, probably.
I listen to what you say,
I watch mannerisms and moves,
Bumperstickers, attire,
Tell me about you,
Much like at the nightclub,
I'll take away your fear,
Make much ado about nothing,
Tell you what you want to hear,
A funnelled line of questioning,
Elicits positive response,
You think that you decided,

Game was cleverly esconced,
As long as you left happy,
You always made my day,
Rush and thrill of closing a deal,
I determined my pay,
This shark's on the beach now,
Flotsam cast ashore by rough seas,
I shake with spasms gasping,
Inner core shaking as I try to breathe,
People feel sympathy,
When there's a whale on the beach,
But sharks get no pity,
You may look but stay out of reach...

11

HOLLOW-POINTS OF HONESTY

HONESTY IS BRUTAL,

TRUTH CAN BE CRUEL,
WE HOLSTER THEM IN LIES,
SAVING THE BLISS OF FOOLS,
WHAT'S WITH THIS CHARADE?
HOW COME THIS GAME IS PLAYED?
SEE IF U CAN SEE BENEATH,
THE TIDES IN WHICH WE WADE,
A LOOK OF ASTONISHMENT,
A MOUTH AGAPE WITH HUSH,
THE PULSE SKIPS A BEAT,
RETURNS A HEATED RUSH,
A GLAZED GAZE STAYS,

A FACE FORCED TO GRIN,
BUT SLACKNESS OF THE POSTURE,
BETRAYS COLLAPSE WITHIN,
ARE THINGS AS THEY APPEAR?
OR WHAT WE WANT TO HEAR?
WHY NOT CUT THE BULLSHIT,
LEST SOMEONE SHED A TEAR,
THE BURDENS ARE A HEAP,
SO SOMEONE ELSE CAN SLEEP,
TOSSING, TURNING, CLINGING TO,
THE SECRETS THAT WE KEEP,
TRUE WORDS CAN HURT AT FIRST,
OR EVEN BRING OUT THE WORST,
THAT'S WHY SOME DANCE DISHON-
ESTLY,
WITH SOULS ABOUT TO BURST,
LET YOUR INNER RAVENS GO,
OR THEY'LL HAUNT YOU LIKE POE,
SCAVENGING THE DEPTHS OF YOU,
AND EVERYONE U KNOW,
TRUTH MAY CHECK YOUR CHIN,
BUT YOU'RE YOURSELF AGAIN,
FEAR MAKES US LIARS,
WHICH IS A COWARD'S SIN.

12

AN OUTSIDE CHANCE
OF FALL

Dukey gazed up at the autumn evening sky as he lay in the tawny fall grass and fiery-colored crunching maple leaves. More were falling slowly, with each rustling breeze.He suddenly realized that he hadn't lain in the grass and looked up at the sky at all since he had been a curly-headed litttle boy. The sun had dropped below the horizon but the clouds were splashed with peach, pink, purplish, and blue hues in the waning light.

Dukey clenched a fistful of the cool grass and ripped it from the earth. He savored the sensation of the brittle blades falling from his fingertips. He watched each exhalation of his frosty breath and was thankful. His eyes closed to see visions in his mind. The fall air triggered a memory.

Locker-room echoes. Cleats scraping on concrete. The smell of earth, turf, and sweat. Sounds of tape being unstrapped. Dingy white painted cinder-block walls. A dusty, ancient, and cob-webbed circulatory system of pipes line the ceiling overhead.

Dukey remembered the warm, salty, metallic taste of blood in his mouth. The grimy busted knuckles. The crackling aching knees. A team of individuals in varying degrees of injury, most of them a bit dazed from smashing into their oppenents, and sometimes each other with all their might. A burly, bespectacled, black man pounding a clipboard who was having none of it.

He had their glassy-eyed, stoic attention. His voice booms filling their subterranean lair under the creaky old stadium.

"But Coach?! But Coach?! I ain't here to talk about what you are doing right. I wanna talk about what we gotta fix...and you know what it is? YOUR ATTITUDE! I ain't gotta go over plays...we been practicing those since last summer. Uh-uh...It's about want to! Yeah they have been getting away with some bullshit but you know what...we're at their house...what the hell did you expect? Complain to ya Mama. They got bleachers full of people who would've stayed home if they thought we were gonna come in here and beat them. LIFE IS NOT FAIR. You gotta make it bend to your will! Block or beat that block! Tackle! Catch! Hold on to the damned ball! Hit! The next time one of those S.O.B.s comes through your gap make sure he goes back to their huddle an inch shorter than when he stuck his nose in Tiger territory! I want them SCARED to shake your hands at the end of this game. You do that and this game will take care of itself! GOT IT?!" Coach Mueller yelled, spittle flying and veins bulging.

Coach should have been a fire and brimstone preacher, but then he wouldn't have been allowed to hit anybody or break stuff. Kids who complained about his gym class would have dis-integrated trying to play football for the man.

"Yeah coach..." was the mumbling collective young men's response. It was obvious that most were reflecting on various misdeeds that the opposing Bears were dishing out to them in the first half.

These included cracking down on the defenders knees so that they were more concerned about injury than tackling. Late bonejarring hits after the whistle, knees to the groin at the bottom of the pile, and occasionally being eye-gouged or stepped on with cleats in the tangled mayhem that was the mechanism of clashing lines of the biggest, fastest, and strongest boys from their respective high schools.

The refs caught some of it, but not most of it. They always saw when you lost your cool and tried to punch or kick somebody in retaliation.

"I SAID DO YOU HAVE IT? I couldn't hear ya..." Coach Mueller boomed his way into their thoughts.

"YEAH COACH!" the young gladiators yelled with building determination.

The call and response yelling and preaching went on for the next five minutes and built in volume, vigor, and violence until helmets were beating against lockers, eyes were focused with a predatory glint, hands were flexing open and closed, legs and feet could not be kept still, and they felt like bees were buzzing around in their stomachs.

"LETS GO GET IT BOYS! TAKE THE FIELD ANDÂ I MEAN TAKE...THE FIELD! LETS GO!"

They all charged out of the tunnel wounds forgotten awash in adrenaline, like the bulls of Pamplona. Their heads were bent, their teeth gnashing, and their faces were masks of bad intentions. Steam charged from their facemasks into the fall night air.

Dukey opened his eyes and thought of that night almost a decade ago. That big old white boy who had been cracking his knees had been caught off guard by how explosive he had launched all his mass and might at him at the first snap of the pigskin after halftime. Dukey didnt usually have fast reflexes and was just put in the middle of the line at nose tackle because he was big and heavy with a meanstreak.

The hit was too perfect. Dukey had slammed all 270 pounds of himself helmet and shoulder first into that big cornbread fed hick's solar plexus and actually stopped his heart right there on the field that night with 11 minutes and 12 seconds left in the third quarter of the game in front the boy's family in the bleachers. A second of triumph and jubilation had been followed by an inhalation of remorse, guilt and horror.   He couldn't remember whether they had won or lost the game.

He had been drinking heavily ever since. Dukey was glad it wasn't going to rain tonight. It was going to be another night sleeping outside homeless. A decade of failed attempts at hustling and managing his anger and inner demons had come to this. The pit. His only solace was that he breathed. In and out. Into the night fall air.
 The hit had been a fall from grace. Dukey knew life wasn't fair. It was just one of those random freak disasters to which his life was prone. This night he struggled to rise. Dukey looked outside at his surroundings and inside himself decided he was not going to sleep under a highway overpass.

The mouthwash which had been his cheap drunk was wearing off.

He gathered himself with creaking joints, dusted himself off, and tried not to bend to his guilt-fueled binging urges. He was numb with cold. A police car slowed and chirped it's siren about half a block away from him.

"Shit. Not these bastards again."

"Hey. You know you can't stay near this greenway. We've been getting complaints from joggers that you've been harassing people for money."

"I gotta eat. Why don't you stop fucking wit me?"

"Alright. You dumb fuck. Get on the ground."

"I ain't botherin' nobody!"

By this time they were out of the cruiser and closing ground on him.

Dukey didn't run, but he didn't get on the ground either. He was still huge. He had never really run from anyone or anything, because he was big and slow.

That's when the pepper spray hit him in the eyes, nose and mouth. He felt like his throat was closing and started to flail blindly around himself.

He connected with one of the cops behind his ear and knocked him sideways. Wrong response.

BLAM!

Game over.

13

MURDERERS ON MY BUS-STOP

Murderers on my bus-stop,
Little did I know,
My peer pressurers included,
A murderers row,
Eating the same candy,
At the same corner-store,
waiting on the same bus,
to take us to class war,
Walked the halls like zombies,
Learning nobody cared,
Fighting over shit like …
Someone scuffed yo kicks or stared,
Busted lips and knuckles,

We hated ourselves,
Sympathy 4 devils,
Like Satan's little elves,
Beat white boys up,
To watch them change colors,
But the most hate and violence,
Was with my black "brothers,"
Murderer number one,
Just seemed a mischievous son,
His sister got school honors,
He really had none,
In a crack-addled rage,
He made headlines first page,
Beat his grandparents to death,
Despite their love and their age,
Murderer number two,
Helped in the robbery and deceit,
Appeared in court as an accomplice,
With shackles on his feet,
Murderer number three,
A hit man for drug-suppliers,
I dont know who he killed,
May be rumors by liars,
4: A hoops King,

Lived right across from the park,
He schooled suckers on his courts,
Till well after dark,
Flyest Jordans filled his closet,
From top to bottom,
Couldnt play for team,
Fuck what a coach taught 'em,
Took mad money from bets,
Swish-jangled chain nets,
Shot a fiend driving off with a rock,
And aint outta jail yet,
Last but not least,
A two for one deal,
My homie got beat by two guys,
And had to keep it real,
He shot them both dead,
Used nine shots of lead,
Emptied magazine and chamber,
In their bodies and heads,
I understand him the most,
You cant let shit like that coast,
Been jumped before too,
Now packing heat wherever I post,
Then people wonder,

About the fakeness of my smile,
And why I lose my goddamn mind,
Every once in a while,
I became what I had to be,
To make it out and survive,
A slippery shape-shifter,
Faking my way thru nine lives,
Its better I suppress,
Lurking murderousness,
When I'll go off…
Even I cant guess,
So envious of the cool,
Who can turn the page,
Grudges like buried mines,
Unintended victims catch rage,
Walking dead like a ghoul,
With a hollowed out soul,
Maybe the only thing I can feel…
Is a wounded leaking hole…
Murderers on my Bus-stop…
drip-drop outlines in chalk,
Murderers on my Bus-stop…
Walked the streets I walked,
Murderers on my bus-stop…

Breathed the poison I breathe,
I see how good your life is,
And I might take it as I seethe…

14

LIFE THROUGH BLUES-COLORED GLASSES

Ahh … the joys of pessimism,
The cynic rarely disappointed,
While optimists reach for the stars,
We snicker at the anointed,
The mind is a sparkling galaxy,
Nestled amidst the darkest of hues,
Life alternates in current,
Between brilliance and the blues,
Blue is the color,
Of the bird of happiness for some,
Blue is the color of asphyxiation,
and what I feel if I'm not numb,
Blue is the color of oxygen-starved blood,

Sluggishly pulsing up my veins,
I gotta take a breath of fresh air,
Until it is revitalized again,
Blues are what you feel,
When you've left your heart unprotected,
And you hold on in pangs of anguish,
As your soul is vivisected,
Blues are the feeling I get,
When my dreams pop like fizz,
"Can I get a tall one and a shot?"
As a blues singer tells it like it is …

15

GULLIBLE

Some have a weakness for,
Belief in fellow man,
Even when tipped off,
RIPPED OFF time and again,
In a world such as this,
How does a dreamer survive?
Connivers calculate and consume,
Devouring suckers alive,
Crushed and ground by molars,
Cut to bits by incisors,
Carcass left looking heavenward,
for luminary advisors,
They smile with straight teeth,
Sharp creases in white collars,

Well manicured smash and grab,
for your fistful of dollars,
Life turns and pivots,
On tiniest of hinges,
Series of feasts and famines,
Self-control and binges,
A sigh of relief,
I wish to breathe,
Crouched defensively,
I lash out and seethe,
Seemed a good idea at the time,
But now pay for your mistake,
Where are your friends and family?
When you buckle or break?

16

Nightmares

I often sigh with relief,
When from these dreams I awake,
Blood spatter, brain matter,
Gurgling sounds the dying make,
Convulsing with gibberish,
Clawing at air,
Darting pupils lose focus,
Glaze over to stare,
If they went down fighting,
Look under their nails,
Or see if they drew blood,
Telling dead men's tales,
I have dreams of torture,
Rounds fired through joints,

Semi-automatic muzzle flashes,
Ligaments exploded by hollowpoints,
The brain wants to live,
The body wants to die,
As if appealing to reason,
I keep hearing "WHY?!?"
Convinced we are strong,
Our bodies are weak,
Vertabrae snap with a twist,
Blades easily spring leaks,
Suicide is just selfish,
Welcome to my hell,
I've watched your so-called lives,
From the abyss in which I dwell,
Even the strongest don't survive,
When cutoff from breath,
Life's one guarantee,
Is randomness of death.

17

A DASH OF HORSEPOWER WITH A TWIST OF TORQUE

Most things in life,
Are a hurry-up-and-wait,
to remedy these begs,
A rip-roaring V-8,
At an on ramp merge,
Succumb to the urge,
to feel thundering herds,
Gallop charging surge,
Mash that hammer down,
Tires squeal and peel,
From inert to projectile,

Muscle launching steel,
There are only 2 types of people,
Those who leave and they who stay,
Redline that beast,
Down the freeway,
A blur of lights,
Ambers, reds, and whites,
And maybe the blues,
If its a bad night,
Some just want transportation,
Boring reliable A to B,
Whats life worth living,
Non-emotion-ally?
Most of the damn critics,

    with pencil-neck ratings and stuff,
    Obviously didnt have to ride,
    The damn bus long enough,
    Women, food, and CARS,
Three Life-long loves,
HOT, fast, and colorful,
Risk is my buzz,
Do you love with your mind?
Or do you love with your heart?
Motown had soul,
We forgot about that part,

Now we sit and wonder:
Where have the blue-collars gone?
Manufacturing base sold,
Former axis powers own,
From a nation full of lenders,
to a nation full of debt,
If we dont take care of our own,
Thats exactly what we get,
Economic warfare is real,
and we are at its crux,
Importing some goods is okay,
But exporting jobs sucks,
So I will continue speeding,
With the banner of lost cause,
to oblivion full throttle,
with a bottle of hot sauce.

18

ARTIST AT WORK

Carving up my canvas,
Ripping up the sketch,
Fixated on a photo,
Leering like a letch,
Obsession: Perfection,
Paint flecks from the brush,
No model no connection,
Still ruin if I rush,
Sleep is death in increments,
These nights I go without,
Mapping outlines and silhouettes,
And shadows of the doubts,
Frame you with my fingers,
Your proportions my perspective,

Quiet storms drown out,
Loudest gales of invective,
Capture you with myriad strokes,
From broad to quick to thin,
Repetitive to fill the space,
But delicately brush your skin,
In midst of night reflecting light,
That illuminates your eyes,
Trace your lips longingly,
Slightly parted breathing sighs,
Hair and tress caress,
Nape of neck brush & flick,
Bring color to your lush face,
And wherever else I pick,
Desire to make you come alive,
And let you sleep no more,
Brush strokes and a painters knife,
So many textures to explore,
Attention paid your details,
From toes to lobes of ears,
Arouse your soul to make you whole,
Until lust for life appears,
Body and palette tensed,
exploring your dimensions,

endorphins rapture,
Inner sensation of ascension,
Not just a scene but a memory,
A moment that takes breath away caught,
And seared into a canvas,
By an artist thinking dirty thoughts,
Some say even Mona Lisa's smile,
Is just a lover's knowing smirk,
Captured for eternity,
By an artist hard at work.

19

YOUR RACE CARD HAS BEEN DECLINED

The problem is we're sorry sir,
Your Race Card's been declined,
You could've used it years ago,
Like Diners Club that time,
For Black Men in America,
A new standard's been set,
White House now black and white,

    Have they stepped up security yet?
You too can be subversive,
by taking care of your kids!
Marry one of your Baby Mamas…
Hey Ladies! Now place your bids!

Yes you too can get A-head,
By paying attention in class,
Great minds don't often rock doo-rags,
Or jeans hanging off their ass,
A Chia head or just ahead,
Act now but wait there's more,
Such an honor you cannot buy,
Offer not available in stores,
To hell with who says you're "acting white,"
When you apply yourself in school,
Learn to speak with proper usage,
Though street-slang is the rule,
When favorite gangsta rappers,
Get out of jail with a felony son,
Likely they have a PTSD,
Can't vote or get a gun,

We all wear uniforms,
Whether we know it or not,
Are you dressed to get a job?
Or a cage, three hots and a cot?
You know we're so sorry sir,
Your Race Card's been declined,
The deck is stacked—life's unfair,
Take a number get in line,

Blood was spilled,
In historic amounts,
But you can't draft,
From forebears' accounts,
Don't act like you can't hustle,
Seen your curbside marketing skills,
The mark-up for profit is less,
But I know you can close deals,
For Black Men in America,
A new standard's been set,
Heres your stop get off the ride,
Hey, are we there yet?
We've got a few more blocks to go,
But give thanks for the lift,
So many before did the grunt work,
Let's bust ass this shift!

20

DRUNK LOGIC

ONE BREW, TWO BREWS,
THREE BREWS, FOUR——
DOUBLE DUECE DRAFTS,
SO I AIN'T GOTTA POUR,
THE USUAL SUSPECTS,
PONTIFICATNG WIT,
MAKING SENSE TO NO ONE ELSE,
EXCEPT A BUZZED LITTLE CLIQUE,
TEQUILA SHOTS, SHOOTER SHOTS,
BREWS FIVE, SIX,
LONG ISLAND ICE TEAS,
MOVING ON 2 MIXED,
BREWS SEVEN, EIGHT,
DAMN, THOUGHT I QUIT,

NEWPORT NUMBER TEN,
CUT MY NICOTINE FIT,
A CANOPY OF HAZE,
STROBES PULSING BLAZE,
THE NIGHT WORE ON,
THE DRINKS POURED ON
UNTIL I WAS A LUNATIC,
A HYPED MO-RON,
FELL BACKWARDS OFF A STAGE,
NO PAIN, DIDN'T MATTER,
STAGGERED UP DANCING,
AS A CROWD GATHERED,
A WILD TIPSY IDIOT,
THINKING LIKE THEY THINK,
THAT WAS SO HILARIOUS,
"I NEED ANOTHER DRINK!"
MY BUDDIES AT THE BAR,
THEY HAD A GOOD LAUGH,
I DASHED TO THE BATHROOM,
YOU CAN DO THE MATH,
WHAT HAPPENED AT THIS POINT,
SUBJECT OPEN TO DOUBT,
I MUST HAVE WALKED AROUND,
BUT I WAS BLACKED OUT,

THINK I WENT TO A PARTY,
MUST'VE BEEN PRETTY GOOD,
WOKE UP WEAVING THRU,
SOME RICH NEIGHBORHOOD,
"WHERE THE HELL AM I GOING?
WHERE THE HELL HAVE I BEEN?
IF YOU GET ME HOME LORD … "
THE DEALMAKING BEGINS,
EYELIDS KEPT CLOSING,
SYRACUSE IN DECEMBER,
NINE DEGREES AND DOZING,
THAT I CAN REMEMBER,
RAN INTO A SNOWBANK,
NEAR 50 MILES AN HOUR,
I'M PRETTY DAMN LUCKY,
OR THERE IS A HIGHER POWER,
ASLEEP AT THE WHEEL,
WHEN THE COPS CAME BY,
TELL 'EM WHAT HE WON BOB:
"IT'S A BRAND NEW——-D.U.I.!"

21

NOVELLA: SHADOW OF A DOUBT #1: KAYNE'S GAMBIT

The Governor's crackberry vibrated with an unavailable listing in the caller screen. His firm and telegenic jaw tightened in anticipation of what to do about his predicament.

Abe Jackson picked up curious and a bit exasperated as he juggled the phone while trying to fasten golden cufflinks through the button-holes at the end of the shirtsleeves of his freshly starched and pressed white linen shirt.

An automated voice intoned: You have a call from an inmate at the Greensville Correctional facility. "Kayne Johnson beeyatch…hahahah… pickup the damn phone you light, bright, almost white muh-fu*ka!"

Do you accept the charges?

"Yes, put him through." Abe winced and said with a weary sigh. "I bet they never let a death row inmate call get through to a white governor." he thought petulantly.

"Whats it gonna be bruh? hahahaha…I got whatchu need…and you got the favor I want. Whassup nucca? Holla at cha boy. Talk to me." Kayne said breezily as if he had a good buzz.

"KJ. I can't be seen to associate with you. NO ONE can know we are kinfolk. I AM sincerely grateful that you would offer to come through for me like this man, but…I just don't know how to play the media if I pardon you." Abe said while nervously massaging his temple with his free hand.

"You MUST be bullshittin' me man. Nigga is you crazy?" Kanyne sneered through the phone. "You NEED my g*ddam kidney!"

"How dare you call ME that! I am the f*cking Governor… I busted my ass to get here. Show some respect." Abe said as he almost pounced from his perch among the files and papers on his desk.

"Typical punkass Abe. Yo ass is always worrying about what people think. F*@K THEM. Ya know... it's funny. We both kingpins... I get deathrow for being one from my side of the tracks... and you get to decide what to do with niggas like me. You gonna do this or what man? Im saving yo dumbass from having to call the witchdoctors at the death-house at three minutes before midnight when they try to shoot me up with that shit. That would be worse publicity. My kidney would do you no good after that and thanks to our HAHAHAHA... incredibly rare ... HAHA... UNIQUE... compatability... If I die... you die... politically and physically." Kayne said with a cold maniacal chuckle.

Abe felt cornered and like his throbbing head would explode. Then he focused and began thinking his way through his response.

"This has to be kept quiet. None of your people outside or inside can know about this. I'll see what I can do. We'll stage it and hide you somewhere else under a new name and social number. BUT... YOU WILL REMAIN on lockdown... I am thinking Utah... out in the middle of nowhere... That governor owes me one....hmmm...we'll make it happen...as long as quiet is kept. The first peep I hear and the deal is off. Then we're both just going to be two more dead black men."

"Yeah...that's my nigga. I knew you was cool in the fan man. That ain't nothing new to me bruh. Shit. The only reason people don't know about us now is I ALREADY got a dead crackhead's name and social... Ima put you up on game man about some shit that you need to know about an asshole you know nothing about who is probably watching both of us... THAT Manipulative mufu*ka..." Kayne whispered hoarsely.

"Who is that?" Abe asked incredulously while rising on his side of the phone.

"Our Frankenstein of a father...he's in the cloned meat industry... I got a story to tell you baby boy." Kayne replied cooly while exhaling smoke from a Newport.

"What?!"

22

NOVELLA: SHADOW OF A DOUBT: #2: COVER YOUR ASS

A pang of anger shot through Abe Jackson's heart. He paced the Governor Mansion's study clenching and unclenching his fist to keep his free hand from shaking as he pressed the mobile phone tightly his ear with the other one. His blood was percolating.

It took all the self-control he could muster to respond calmly to the brother who was the insidious liability that Abe's rivals would most assuredly use to destroy him in elections. He had his own personal Willie Horton for a sibling. That is if his enemies or even allies ever found out about the damned brotherly connection.

"You're lucky I believe only God can judge people worthy of life and death. If anybody deserves the death penalty It's YOU. Don't you dare disparage our deceased father you deranged ingrate. You are not out of the woods yet. I might still change my mind and let them execute you. Just so you know, as soon as I get off of this phone I am going to have my medical staff search even more intently all over this country to find a compatible kidney donor for me. I pray every night that I get one from anybody but you. I am sure you gave Dad his stroke with your stupid shit. On top of that, I'm sure that Mama died of a broken heart thinking that she could've saved you if Daddy hadn't had to kick you out. Kenneth Jackson III. You are a disgrace." Abe said, through clenched teeth.

"You know what muthaf**ka? Fu*k you! I'm Kayne! You betta recognize nigga. One of my little girlfriends on the outside might surprise you. Watch where you get yo haircut on the campaign trail nigga, hahaha! What if I told you someone had sent some of your hair or manicure clippings to a geneology service along with mine? hahahaha! Just to keep yo sneaky lawyah ass honest! We can get on some Jerry Springer gangsta shit if you wanna gamble in a game that you can't play playa! HAHHA! Don't you know who you dealing wit? I DO! You punkass weasel.

I suggest you figure that out boy. CHECK-MATE beeatch!" Kayne hissed into the phone and slammed it against the wall and walked off.

Kayne Johnson was the living and breathing skeleton in his family's closet. Fortunately for Abe, KJ had exchanged identity with a dead mentor dealer and crackhead (who he had killed and put in a 55 gallon drum full of gasoline and oil and burnt beyond ID), out of hatred for his father and when on the run from the DEA, ATF, FBI, and the IRS. His tactics to rise to the top of and to expand the drug weight moving and gun-running clique called T- DOWN were the stuff of gruesome street legend.

Kayne Insane's actions and edicts were unflinching enough to earn the new fake Kayne Johnson a spot on death-row after three former T-Downers copped pleas and snitched on him for reduced sentences. They had all been killed since that time.

Songbird one's throat was punctured by a sharp, filed down end of a hard plastic toothbrush handle at lunchtime in lock-up. SING NOW was smeared on his chest in blood apparently with the blunt rounded end of the same home-made shank. There were no fingerprints because the handle was found melted stuck to the heating element of a bun toaster in the kitchen later that day. No witnesses. Video just showed the rat disappearing under a group of about ten inmates for about 45 seconds, before they hurriedly dispersed in scattershot directions. Most that were identified were lifers.

Another rat had apparently fell, and repeatedly hit his head against the shower wall and floor until he died from brain hemorrhaging. SHOWER SINGER, was scratched into his skin by some unidentified sharp object. Still, there were no witnesses to be found. C.O.s were always strangely absent when these incidents occurred.

The most damaging plea bargainer, Jake, had made it out of Kayne's prison unscathed and early. He met his end with his own suicidal trigger-pull after discovering his two little girls had been threatened at gunpoint. They were told of the T-Downers expectation of their father, as they jumped rope double-dutch on the sidewalk, by Kayne's top enforcer, Lieutenant Rent. Tejas or Tay Renteria who wanted either money, gang loyalty, or respect no matter what always due like rent in front of their grandma's project apartment building, when his babies' mama came to pick Jake up on the day of his release.

Abe Jackson had followed his disowned older sibling's career with horrified interest. Kayne's sins mounted to the heavens.

Abe threw his mobile phone across the room in frustration. It clattered across his desk, and buried itself amidst a pile of documents and papers with a rustle. He immediately ran over to retrieve it and began tossing papers this way and that until he found his prize and nemesis.

"GET ME DOCTOR SISKEL! Right now." He commanded the cell on speakerphone. Abe held his head in hands and rocked back and forth sitting on the edge of his chaotic desk.

23

NOVELLA: SHADOW OF A DOUBT #3: Pieces In Motion

After getting a frantic call from Abe Jackson, Dr. Abraham Siskel sat leaning upon his elbows at his desk with bony fingers interlocked and clasped. He rested his wrinkled, craggy chin atop his papery , translucent knuckles with his salt-pepper bushy eyebrows knitted together across his furrowed liver-spotted brow. He was deep in thought murmuring to himself and occasionally scratching his old, balding head.

Abe's namesake had befriended Ken Jackson Jr. when he was still doing graduate work at the University of Utah on helping map the human genetic code and doing cloning research afterwards for organ harvests to offset lack of donors and immune system rejection challenges.

Befriending the obsessive man was probably an over-statement. Dr. Ken was unemotional to the point of often behaving like an automaton. He had tunnel-vision once he started upon a project. His scientific accomplishments were mind-blowing because of his dedication and focus. Dr. Ken had married a woman that he selected because of her intelligence and maternal instincts, not love, of which he seemed incapable.

Doc Siskel shook his head thinking about the Jackson boys. Dr. Ken's family life was a story of absentee neglect. Little Abe had looked up to his Dad like he was the genius that he was. Abe sought his Dad's attention by seeking academic heights comparable to the man. Doc remembered the little curly-headed, bucktoothed beaming face of a skinny little bi-racial boy running around showing the gold stars and A+s on his papers to anyone who would look.

The firstborn son Ken Jackson III grew to despise how much his Dad stayed away at his work. He hated the man's successes.

KJIII actually laughed aloud when he discovered his quivering naked mother in the throes of passion on the living room floor being pounded with piston like pumping of the hilariously hairy buttocks of a trouser-less insurance salesman who had kept stopping by long after selling the policy. She was the first person he ever blackmailed for money. He was 11 years old.

Doc Siskel was the only member of his family's friends that KJIII liked and got along with. He found the watery-eyed son of Holocaust survivors empathetic to his feelings. Those dark eyes glistened when he laughed and looked like he would cry when you told him what was troubling you. It was kind of a curse because it always got him nominated to give patients bad news, but made him beloved whether he was sincere or not.

Siskel was amazed at how smart the kid who became Kayne was. He listened to the boy's concerns about world affairs and social inconsistencies when he was only 8 years old and getting mood swings.

What KJIII really liked to do with Old Doc, as he called him, was to play chess. Doc laughed at how fast KJIII moved in for the kill and had no qualms about sacrificing pieces recklessly to get the checkmate. What the Doc really was impressed with was that the preadolescent Kayne could play on his level, but only when he held his volatile emotions in check.

The funniest chess memory was when Doc had set up a match between Little Abe and KJIII. As was typical of him, the younger sibling had read up on openings, tactics, defenses and was holding his own pretty well against Kayne. The elder son was very much chagrined. The funny thing was how slow, deliberate, and calculating little Abe was, which had the fast and loose playing Kayne going beserk yelling: "GIMME a TIMED game! Put his ass on the clock!" A stale-mate was averted when KJIII upset the table and sent chess pieces flying across the floor in every direction.

Kayne occasionally still wrote the old fellow from jail. Sometimes there were teardrop spatters in the ink on the paper. The affection was dangerous. It was common knowledge around town that anyone who sued the old doctor for malpractice would get an immediate bounty put on their liver. Because in Kayne's words, "If you bring me muhfu*kas liver, they aint living."

Doc Siskel seemed to have made his mind up about something and then awkwardly scooted his wheeled office-chair over to his computer, squinted through his spectacles, and began hesitantly pecking and tapping at the keyboard.

Contact:kj2prof@dna/blkops/dod/harvest-proj.gov

PASSWORD: LAZARUS1970

Message: Two principals @ critical mass. Principal A compromised by principal K. Principal A REQUIRES renal harvest supplement to avert Principal K rapid entrapment and endgame. All other avenues and sources exhausted and unsatisfactory to acquire renal supplement. Both Principals may be terminated unless action taken now.

Reply: Have required renal supplements in inventory. Right or left? DO NOT Inform Principal A until pardon and relocation for Principal K is completed. No contact between principals to be permitted post-op until further notice. Inform Principal A renal harvest supplement is from

Principal K. Inform principal K that renal harvest supplement from him is not required therefore making him expendable. Supplements in regenerative inventory 99.95% compatible and rejection risk near nil. PROCEED and debrief me upon completion.

Message: They need you. Cut the principals crap DR. I am glad you condescended to save them both. I ought to tell Abe about you. I am tired of being the rickety old pawn and liason between you and yours. F.Y.I. kj3 suspects you are alive and what you are doing. I don't know how, but his tentacles seem to go into some tiny cracks.

Reply: KJ3 does not exist. KAYNE does by his choice. He is defective and must be forced into a corrective mold. Abe is under my watchful eye and guardianship. DO NOT PRESUME to pontificate to me about how I handle family affairs. I have a higher calling and family just gets in the way of my life-saving research and creations. My actions were necessary.

Message: How does it feel to play GOD?
Reply: ?

24

NOVELLA: SHADOW OF A DOUBT #4: A DISTANT FATHER

An aged man with an angular face and a high and broad forehead sat in a mobile office chair in front of one of his legion computer monitors. A pallid, deathly blue-ish glow from the screen cast his sharp features into jagged shadowed relief in a darkened laboratory.

The gray-haired researcher's posture was erect and his long orthopedic shoes were flat on the pale waxed ceramic floor beneath him. He clattered away at an ergonomic keyboard with his spindly fingers. The man would do this in stops and starts after peering over his half-lenses reading responses. The secluded patriarch of the exceptional Jackson clan finally stopped and stroked his smooth chin with a slightly puzzled look on his usually emotionless face. Calculating gray eyes stood out in contrast to his pecan complexioned skin.

Dr. Kenneth Jackson Jr. was unsure of what to make of his confidant and close associate, Doc Siskel's last online query.

Message: "How does it feel to play GOD?"

Dr. KJ was irked by this line of questioning. Siskel was getting too emotional about the boys situation. He finally replied:

"?"

The thought alone of belief in a supreme Deity irritated him. Dr. KJ thought of all the money that went into organized religion's collection plates and coffers.

"For what?" he thought, "Some soothing bedtime stories while people die every day waiting for organs. At least I could give them something for their money. LIFE. Nooo, no, let's give it to a bunch of quacks, snake-oil pharmaceutical companies, and preachers so they can buy McMansions and Mercedes-Benzs."

It was one of the few subjects that angered him.   His funding was drying up. Politicians railed against the idea of cloning humans for harvest organs, and actually put laws in effect to that end. The technology was in place for human cloning, and had been for over a decade. He hated emotional responses.

It was logical that the perfect organ donors for patients were THEMSELVES. Minimal risk of rejection. The only obstacle to that solution was if they were genetically defective and their organs were the problem, and not the result of lifestyle choices. Dr. KJ was working on genetic modifications to flank that obstacle.

His operations had been forced underground but were secretly being funded by a Department of Defense black ops program. The military had understood the value of having expendable and interchangeable parts. If China or some other extremely populous military threat arose, the military knew that they would have to stretch their soldiers further by swapping a spare organ in, and sending the repaired unit back into the fight.

Now the fickle military was more interested in nanotechnology, automated killers, cyber-weapons, satellite weapons, and gee-wizardry in general. Dr. KJ's plan to use military funding to benefit mankind was in need of a plan B.

Dr. KJ swiveled around slowly in his chair and looked around at his dimly lit subterranean work area. Servers and LED lights winked at him. Microscopes, test-tubes, a battle line of computers and monitors, and various otherworldly instruments and mechanized devices lined the perimeter of drab white walls. Ominous looking ranks and files of super-cooled containers labeled: ORGAN INVENTORY glinted dully from behind a plexi-glass wall.

The frustrated doctor had given up his family for the good of mankind only to betrayed by an ambivalent military. This laboratory was all he had to show for his life's work.

Dr. KJ thought of his boys and retrieved old faded photo portraits of them in their toddler years from his wallet. Their mother had dressed them in matching tiny three piece suits for their portrait day. Abe's was dark blue, and Kayne's was dark grey. He traced his delicate thumb across the photo of Little Abe's gray-eyed smiling face. A tear tracked its way slowly down his cheek unbeknownst to him.

Then he held up Kayne's photo. That little, curly-headed, green-eyed miscreant, who did not deserve the name Kenneth Jackson III. He had to avert his eyes from Kayne's unemotional stare from the photograph. He felt like the image was watching him for a weakness.

"I may have a use for you my son. You may redeem yourself yet." He murmured under his breath and clasped them both to his heart.

25

NOVELLA: SHADOW OF A DOUBT #5: AN EVENING ALONE WITH KAYNE

Kayne lay in his cot staring up at the top bunk. His mind raced trying to connect the dots to the recent series of events. His bloodshot eyes burned and itched, but he could not sleep. He had the nervous energy of a panther with its paw clamped in a trap.

He had watched his brother smoothly tap-dance his way through a press conference in heavy TV make-up, a tailored Savile Row suit, and a power tie. Abe Jackson had projected power, with perfect diction, proper emphasis at key points, and strong gestures. Abe concluded with a sanctimonious flourish in Kayne's pardon, or reduction of sentence, or whatever the hell this was.

"I cannot stand idly by while this man is put to death. My decision as governor of this great state, is due to discrepancies in the DNA evidence, mislabeling of some samples, and outright disappearance of others, in addition to the lack of surviving eyewitnesses who were shaky at best. Kayne Johnson's victims can take comfort in the fact that he will have a lifetime behind bars to pay his debt to society. In addition, he will be transferred to a maximum security prison in another state to protect local inmates from his organization and influence. I will not take questions at this time. God bless you and good-night."

Then, Abe had confidently strode away from the press conference room podium, and nearly collapsed behind the curtains after he was out of the view of the cameras. He was immediately whisked away by medical staff in order to receive a much needed kidney transplant.

Kayne was out of his sphere of influence. None of his homeboys were in this lockup. These mormon C.O.s seemed to take their jobs too seriously. The former kingpin was sure that money would crack them eventually. Everybody has a price. It was just taking too long. He hated the fact that he would have to start a new network here from the ground up. Kayne had nothing, except time to think.

"Nice touch baby bruh, you goody-two shoes little prick." He growled under his breath, through an intense scowl. "Utah?! Lily white Utah. In the middle of the damned desert. Not enough brothas here to take over and run this joint. Gonna have to hook it up with the essays. Tay Rent is the ace up my sleeve with that. Yeah, same little Abe! Pretty slick. Still, sneaky as ever. I knew I should have asked for more, but he ended up not taking my kidney anyway."

What mystified Kayne was a memo that he had received from an anonymous source during his transfer to a supermax prison in Utah. His brother no longer needed his kidney because a more compatible match donor had been found. More compatible than his brother?

"Why didn't he let me be executed?" Kayne wondered somewhat thankfully. "I know what I would've done." he almost snickered to himself. "He always was sooo f*cking soft. hahaha." he actually chuckled.

Then to add to Kayne's bewilderment, he had received a letter from his little brother, Abe, under an alias that thanked him profusely for donating his organ to save him.

"Who would want to hustle the both of us? I know this ain't no accident. Who's running this game?" he asked himself repeatedly, while he supported his weight with his arms extended behind him and his palms flat on the edge of his metal cot. He extended his legs with knees bent as if sitting, and proceeded to furiously perform dip exercises up and down. His breath came out in snorts and hisses. His mind wandered into scattered arenas of possibility. For some reason his mind slowed to a somewhat funny memory of his father.

It had been an evening at a pool hall and nip joint that sold watered down gin in paper cups for a dollar. It was on the bottom floor of a decrepit two-story boarding house that Kayne lived in after his expulsion from the Jackson home.

15 year old Kayne had been hustling games from suckers after letting them win a few initial games, then getting them to really ante up, and clearing the table, with sudden skilled shots. The old crazy coot to which Kayne bore a strong resemblance had showed up in a freaking lab jacket. The old man wanted him to come back home.

The prodigal son, for his part, wanted to wipe the pool table with his nerdy father. His Dad had played around with him a little and attempted weak jokes and strained attempts at conversation.

"Let's make this interesting old man, wanna play for a few bucks?" Kayne had asked slyly.

"I don't think that would be advisable young man." His Dad had replied somewhat nervously, looking around at the hoodlums who were arguing loudly, and about to come to blows at the next table.

"Come on, live a little. It'll be fun. That's why we don't get along. Loosen up man!" Kayne had replied leaning on his favorite pool stick.

"Umm, okay. Just one game. Let's make this quick." Dr. Ken said biting his lip and surveying the angles of the table. The pervasive cigarette, cigar, and weed smoke in the liquor laced confined space, obviously bothered his eyes and made him cough and wheeze.

"Don't worry! I will pops." Kayne had laughed.

Much to his embarrassment, his dorky Dad had proceeded to wipe the table clean with shot after shot after Kayne broke the balls. Hustlers stared at the tall thin man using trigonometric equations aloud to call his shots. Kayne was furious and humiliated because his little gang of new "friends" had decided to watch and laid down bets. He didn't even get a chance to shoot.

"This game is about setting up the next shot. Not the easy or quick one. You've got to think multiple shots ahead for success here and in the world." His irritating Dad preached at him.

"I guess spending all your time in a batcave in the ground is yo idea of success. Git the f*ck outta here. Go back to your hole old man. Take this!" Kayne called, throwing balled up dollars after him, as he exited hurriedly into the night.

Kayne launched himself upright when the one
and only possible answer came to him. "Pops."
Sweat beaded his forehead as he stood shaking
his head and pounding a fist into his palm. Veins
bulged from his pumped arms and shoulders as
he seethed. The thought occurred to him that
his obsessive father had access to the legal and
criminal powers of his sons, if his father was
indeed alive. The man would control all aspects
of the game from his lair in the labyrinth and
shadows. Kayne had to find out for certain. He
felt like a madman's plaything.

"Ahahhhaaayyyaaarrgaahhaaah!!! Just wait till
I find you! AAAAIIIIAAAHHH-
HUUUGGGHHH!" he yelled while repeatedly
slamming his body against the bars and alter-
nately beating the cinderblock walls with his fists,
until his knuckles were bruised, scraped, and
bleeding.

26

NOVELLA: SHADOW OF A DOUBT #6: Unrequited Brotherly Love

Governor Abe Jackson lay in his hospital bed recovering from his recent kidney transplant. He was in visceral pain but could feel his strength returning to him by the hour. In his sedated cloudy-headed state, his thoughts floated in and out of clarity.

"Thank God for no more dialysis..ugghhh."

An unfamiliar feeling consumed him. Abe missed his brother for the first time since he was a child. Abe wept silently with gratitude. He couldn't get over the fact that the sibling who he denied and shunned had saved his life, or so he thought.

Abe's memory floated back to the bedroom he had shared with his brother when they were little kids, before Dad had got a huge military medical research contract, and had moved the family to a big house in the hills.

The boys used to kneel at their bedsides and pray every night, before they got into their un-stacked bunk-beds on either side of their little, tacky room. KJ perfunctorily recited the same prayer every night, but Abe had really prayed. He would ask God for stuff, and pray for his brother and his family, sometimes at length, as KJ watched incredulously.

Abe used to beg his 15-month older sibling to tell him stories after Mom had kissed them good-night and turned off the light and left them to go down the hall to her ever-present friends, com-panions, and sometimes, even her husband.

KJ was a masterful story-teller. He would just make stuff up off the top of his head. KJ was so believable and convincing because he seamlessly mixed fact and fiction. KJ whispered tales across the room until his little brother stopped asking questions and giggling, and fell asleep drooling on his pillow.

Abe smiled at the long-forgotten memory that had popped into his head.

"When was the last time I thought of KJ and smiled?" he wondered aloud.

It didn't matter to him that Kayne had attempted to barter a kidney to save himself quid pro quo with the governor who was secretly his brother to get a stay of execution. It was a ruse to hide familial emotions as far as he was concerned.

Abe knew he would never let ANYBODY be executed on his watch as governor anyway. He was sure KJ knew that already. His opposition to the death penalty had nearly cost him a hotly contested election in his blue-dog Democrat and Red-dog Republican skirmishing southern state. KJ didn't strike him as someone who feared or gave a damn about death.

"How could this be? A murderer, drug-dealer, pimp, gunrunner, scourge of the northwest side of the city, a condemned man just gave of himself, to save me? My brother, oh my brother, I will never understand you KJ, never." He mumbled while closing his eyes.

Abe was such an optimist and positive thinker that he chose to dwell on the value of the gift and the self-sacrifice that he thought had been required of the brother who had been clinically diagnosed as a sociopath at age 12. A sociopath feels nothing for anyone and operates solely out of self-interest. Abe chose to believe that KJIII wanted him to live. It made his brother human. He wanted him to be.

Abe remembered the pained expression that always contorted his mother's face whenever she interacted with KJIII. Bette was an artist and musician, who was extremely emotional and empathetic to most people. KJ seemed to scare her. People were drawn to her, but Kayne wasn't. She was loved by most who met her almost immediately. Her intelligence shone in every conversation, and she was a great listener. She savored fine wines with her art-house pals but was not above swilling beer with her musician buddies.

Mother had always looked for the best in people. She and Abe had been very close, but

KJIII's anti-social behaviors and violent tendencies seemed beyond her comprehension and reach. Dr. Ken often blamed his wife for Kayne's misbehavior.

"You don't even work. All you have to do is give that boy some discipline and structure and he'll come around. He's smart. You must be doing something wrong. Be a parent for goodness sake. I have to work to provide for this family. All I ask is that you take care of these kids. Why can't you even do that adequately? Sometimes I think I never should have married you." He had often told her coldly, as she sobbed.

Bette was a tragic figure in Abe's memory. She had always talked to Little Abe like he was a grown-up. It was apparent from heartfelt talks between her and Abe when she was lonely, and that she had thought that she could change the Jackson boys' father before she had impulsively married him. She had been rebellious, idealistic, and fresh out of liberal-arts college. The good doctor stayed away at work and demanded that she stay with the kids. She was like a caged bird with beautiful plumage that was robbed of the joys of flight.

Mom was not a perfect woman. She had often slacked on cleaning and straightening up around the house because she just wasn't an orderly person, much to her obsessive-compulsive husband's consternation. Her artistic soul tended to just go with the flow. Begrudgingly, he had hired a maid.

Bette was beautiful, with creamy skin, smoky hazel eyes, and a chestnut-colored mane, but she had low self-esteem. She could not always resist flattery and advances from lecherous men who paid attention to her, because of her romantic starvation and reading too many harlequin romance paperbacks. Little Abe turned a blind eye to her indiscretions, but KJIII meticulously catalogued her infidelity. Her weight tended to fluctuate from plump to skeletal and anorexic-looking. Her mental ups and downs, from manically depressed bed-ridden lows to endorphin overdosed frenzies of artwork, composing, and exercising activity, were unpredictable.

Abe missed her more than his Dad. There was only one hurtful thing he could remember her doing. He had peeped around a corner into their kitchen as KJIII and his mother argued. The boy who became Kayne didn't really argue. From a young age, he maintained an expressionless impassive demeanor and broke his mother down by harping on every mistake in her logic, speech, and inserted insults, to get her emotional and off-balance, in a ruthless attempt to win and make her look stupid.

"IT'S SO HARD TO LOVE SOMEBODY WHO ACTS AND LOOKS SO MUCH LIKE SOMEONE YOU HAAAATE!" Bette had shrieked at him and snatched up a cast-iron skillet with trembling hands as if she wanted to bust him one in the face with it.

Young KJIII had looked her in the eye and smiled.

Bette had shuddered, dropped the skillet on the linoleum floor, and stormed off down the hall breaking porcelain knick-knacks, and knocking books off of shelves along the way, to drink her-self into oblivion.

Abe suddenly felt the urge to pray for KJ. That boy had never been quite right since Abe had accidentally knocked him down a flight of stairs at their old house, as their mother slept. They had been taking turns jumping down the stairs, going up higher a step each time, until they finally were at the top step. KJ lost his nerve just before the last jump and Abe gave him a slight push. He had felt guilty about KJ ever since.

KJ had hit the concrete floor below face-first and suffered a double concussion when his brain slammed into the front of his skull and bounced internally to hit the back of his skull. KJ had struggled to his feet with two black eyes, a busted lip, and a huge swollen hematoma on his forehead, crying and screaming uncontrollably. He was six. Abe was 4 and a half.

The elder sibling had never been the same. KJ was still smart, just odd and conniving most of the time.Â It was then and afterwards, that Dr. Ken had started calling KJIII defective.

"I've got to help him.Â For if you do not forgive men their trespasses, neither will your heavenly Father forgive your trespasses." Abe thought to himself, quoting Matthew 5:15.

27

NOVELLA: SHADOW OF A DOUBT #7: REALITY CHECK

"I want to thank him personally Doc. I just feel so much better. There is no way I can repay him, but I just want go see him and show him how much I appreciate what he did to save his long-lost little brother. Maybe he has found God in prison or something. Maybe he is changing his life in his isolation. I gotta go at least give him a hug or put some money in his commissary or something. We have to nurture this side of him before it disappears!" Governor Abe Jackson gushed to his mentor over the phone.

"Absolutely NOT!" Doc Siskel replied with alarm, suddenly raising his rickety old frame from his reclining easy chair in his study, and nearly spilling his cognac.

"Easy there. Calm down before you have an aneurysm. I can hear you knocking stuff around over there." Abe chuckled. "Look man. I know I agreed to the stips that there could be no contact with the donor, but that's my brother, man. Thanks for the kidney sucker. Enjoy rotting the rest of your natural born life in a cell with no contact with the outside world. What kind of bullshit is that? This was so out of character for him. I would've thought he would gladly watch me suffer and die waiting on a kidney. I mean, well, you how he is…or was! This just needs some kind of positive reinforcement man. I've got to go see him. It's the least I can do." Abe reasoned, as if delivering a sales pitch.

Doc Siskel took a slow puff of one of his beloved Sancho Panzas. He composed himself, and shook his goblet in a slow circular motion to swirl his drink, and then attempted a more nuanced tack with Abe. "Have you forgotten who KJ is Abe? Hell, he tried to feed you to your next-door-neighbors' German Shepherd dog when you were five. THAT was BEFORE he got a criminal record. His behavior hasn't exactly progressed in a positive arc since then. I understand that you are grateful. You know KJ and I were close, but he was always an unpredictable and conflicted person. Let's be realistic here. This donation, even though positive, is either consistently unpredictable, or just a way to save his own neck. Not to mention the fact, that you would be cast out of the Governorship of this state, if the media found out that the murderer and drug kingpin that you granted a stay of execution turned out to be, secretly, your brother. You increase the chances of your family ties being discovered every time you contact him. That's just the way it is. Be reasonable Abe. It's sweet of you to want to reach out to him, but it's still extremely dangerous. Think about it."

Abe guffawed, "Oh man! You had to really dig down deep for that one Doc. Man! I had almost forgotten about that little incident! HAHA-HAHA! Hey nobody put a gun to my head.

HAHAHA, you kill me! KJ just said he would give me the rest of his bag of sour tarts if I went and got the ball he had kicked into the neighbors' yard. Bruno's eyes opened and that big head popped up as soon as I touched the ball. I saw the hair stand up on his back! Heehehee... mine probably did too! Man! I never ran so fast in my life! That dog was moving boy! HAHAHAH! You gotta admit that was kinda funny Doc. Give me a break. KJ was just playing around."

"Abe, maybe you were too young to realize it, but Bruno, I guess you call him, was a trained attack and guard dog. It was so well-trained that Mr. Bud didn't need a fence, unless someone entered the perimeter of his backyard. KJ didn't know the neighbor was there, to call him off from chasing you, from his window. I hate to think what would've happened if he had caught you. He would have too, you know. You were lucky that you screamed so loud that you woke his owner. Bud worked nights, and was a day-sleeper." Doc recalled with weariness.

"You think KJ was trying to kill me then? Cmon Doc! We were kids being kids man. It had to have been a sight! That dog chased me through the garden and down the alley, and that rascal KJ had eaten all the candy by the time I got back to him. He was laughing so hard that he was crying! He had watched the whole thing from our back-porch. I was such a sucker little brother." Abe giggled.

"KJ never called for help for you, did he? I never told you what I'm going to say to you now." Old Doc paused, sighed on his end of the phone, and took a deep sip of his cognac to steel his resolve.

"Well say what you've to say Doc. Spit it out. We're grown folks here." Abe said, impatiently.

"Once, KJ wrote me, that he would've laughed just as hard if that Alsatian had caught you. You know, he never forgave you for the accident. That man never loses a grudge. At least, as far as I know, and for the entire time that I have known him. We're talking since childhood Abe. Don't fool yourself. I doubt isolation has been good for a mind like that. Trust me when I tell you this. It's a bad idea. Take a breath. Give things some time, Abe. Let the media cool down about the pardon and I'll do what I can to help. He still writes me. I'll have to show you what I'm talking about. I hate to betray his trust, but it is for your own good. Be careful. Hell, I'm scared to tell KJ not to write me about his murders, maimings, scores to settle, drug and gun deals gone bad, paranoias, and the nightmares. Good God! The dreams! I'm scared to see him, and he actually likes me." Doc Siskel, cautioned, palming his haggard face with a wrinkled hand.

"Okay. Okay. I got it. I'm still gonna send him a letter and some money or something. You say seeing him is a bad idea, but I feel like I am missing a perfect opportunity to make things good between us again." Abe sulked.

"How did you make it this far in politics being such a Pollyanna?" Doc Siskel couldn't help but chuckle in Abe's ear.

"People are drawn to positive people, and people can change." Abe contended defensively.

"Things haven't been good between Kayne and ANYBODY for longer than you know, Governor." Doc Siskel said with certainty, and crushed his cigar ash with a grimace, before hanging up the phone. He felt like a traitor, and a puppet of Abe and KJ's father, the clandestine Dr. Ken.

28

NOVELLA: SHADOW OF A DOUBT #8: DADDY BRINGS A KIDDIE KAYNE TO WORK DAY

"Son, do you know why Little Abe pushed you down the steps?" an uncharacteristically smiling Dr. Ken Jackson Jr. asked a distracted six year old KJII.

"I donno. Abe said he was sorry. Why are you laughing at me? It's not funny. It hurts."

KJIII's face looked like he had been in a car-wreck, and he held an ice pack on his bandaged forehead. His swollen lips were cracked and blood-stained.

The little boy's bloodshot and blackened eyes were widening open as he looked around his Dad's research lab. He tried to take in blinking LED lights, whirring disk drives, disembodied automated computer voices that occasionally spoke, bright ranks and files of LCD monitors, shimmering plexi-glass wall panels leading off into dark corridors with incubators, robotic arms, centrifuges, microscopes, stacks of containers smoking with dry ice, and four large horizontal stainless steel boxes with double doors atop 4-wheeled gurneys were under spotlights in an adjacent room with respirators and two operating tables, and lots of odd-looking things the kid couldn't comprehend.

This bizarre inner sanctum was under an abandoned old church, and could only be accessed by going through a hermetically-sealed door and anti-bacterial/microbial mist in the basement of the former rectory.

Dr. Ken leaned in close to KJIII's battered face, and gave him a wink over his half-lenses, "I'm not laughing at you son. Everything happens for a reason, whether you know it or not. My best guess is that deep down, AJ wants to replace you as prince of the hill. You are my first-born son. I'll tell you a secret KJ. You have a gift that seems to always be bestowed upon a patriarchal Jackson. Detachment, and an analytical mind without the regard for social conformity. No matter how hard he tries, Abe can never change the fact that YOU are the pre-eminent future leader of this family, and if things go according to plan, quite possibly, the heir to my life's work and knowledge that WILL change human history."

"Whatcha mean Daddy?" the young boy asked as he hopped down from the rotating tall metal stool burning with desire to explore the other-worldly workplace.

"Don't go touching anything around here. Heck, I have a computer that's been crunching the solution to a same algorithmic sequence for three and a half years. The last thing I need is for you to accidentally hit that key. Sit back down, I'm talking to you! Don't you want to know what makes you special? Hang on. Sit back, watch this . I will show you something cool if you promise to hear me out afterwards. Deal?"

"OOOhh! You've got an animal room! Cool! Can I go play with some of them?" KJ exclaimed, bouncing on his tip-toes and wiggling his fingers.

"No! I mean, I don't think that's a good idea. Most are kind of works in progress. I try to make the best of them grow bigger and tastier at an accelerated rate of growth. They aren't normal animals and many responses are species atypical aggression. Just sit. Please."

"Okay, Daddy." A disheartened little explorer replied with a sigh, and climbed back atop his perch on a shiny metal swivel stool.

Dr. Ken keyed a remote controller and the lab's ceiling slowly parted into slotted recesses along the perimeter of the room, to reveal the high-arched dark stained wood-beamed rafters of the old church ceiling above them through a plexi-glass enclosure pane. The church's mosaic stained glass oculus facade window bathed the vaulted space above them in a kaleidoscope of light rays and dust particles. A flock of pigeons that had found a way in to nest in the old church began fluttering around nervously because of the disturbance beneath them.

The tall lanky man in the lab coat stood close, and put an arm on the bandaged kid's shoulder.

They grinned together for a moment and beamed upwards.

"Cool huh?"

"Yeah, Pop."

"Alright, let's close this up before those birds crap all over the glass." Dr. Ken said, and hurriedly hit the close button.

"Awww, man. That was quick." KJ whined.

"I'm going to tell you a story young man. A deal is a deal. Now that I have your attention, let's begin." Dr. Jackson said, professorially.

KJ rested his elbows on a tabletop and leaned towards his Dad, and gave him his best "I'm interested" look, despite a slight pout. He was mystified at how nice his Dad was acting today.

KJ was glad that his Dad had brought him to work with him for once.

He had never thought such a boring, absent, and quiet father, could spend all his time in such an awesome place as this secret laboratory.

"My field of study is genetics/reproduction and organ regeneration research. Do you know what that means?" the scientist asked.

"No." KJIII said, fidgeting.

"Your little brother still plays with that Mr. Potato Head doll doesn't he?"

"Yep."

"What if I told you that you can change people the same way you can change that doll? For example, if something is wrong with their eyes, you can put a different pair in."

"You can do that?" KJIII asked, looking puzzled.

"Yes, but you have to have a spare that fits them like your puzzle pieces. Everybody is a unique puzzle. My idea is that if you make a spare entire Mr. Potato Head from the same mold, or copy the entire puzzle, you will always have the parts and pieces you need to fix sick people." the doctor said, interlocking his fingers.

"Is that cheating?" KJIII asked, with a squint.

"I'm saving people's lives by cheating. If that's what you want to call it. In this case, if you aren't cheating, you aren't trying hard enough. It is life and death, son." Dr. Jackson said, with a penetrating gaze.

"What about the second Mr. Potato Head? Doesn't it hurt him to take stuff off of him to put

on the first one? I would be mad if I was him."
the kid said, looking down and away.

"He doesn't count, because he is just for spare
parts." Dr. Jackson said, firmly.

"That's still not fair—" KJIII stopped mid-sen-
tence. His eyes, which had continued to scan the
lab, were fixed on something dimly shimmering
behind Dr. Ken in one of the darkened rooms
down the corridor. The usually impassive face of
the boy looked terrified.

"Daddy I'm scared, is that a blue lady floating
in that water-tank down the hall? She looks like
she's sleeping with her eyes open. She looks like
Mama."

29

NOVELLA: SHADOW OF A DOUBT #9: THE BACKWARDS PAWN

"There is nothing to fear, my son. That is a prototype of a harvest pod. It is not a person. Your mother, NOT MAMA, is fine. Isn't it magnificent? She is the apex of health science and life-saving technology of the future. She is the first of her kind." Dr. Ken said calmly, with a nonchalant wave of a hand.

"Well it sure looks like Ma! I mean mother. Why is she blue, and in that water tank?" She looks like she is floating up dead. I don't want to see her anymore. You did something bad, didn't you Daddy?" KJ had said tearing up, and giving his Dad an accusatory glance, and then looked away. He was angry and scared.

"CALM DOWN! Look at me when I'm talking to you! Where is your ability to reason? Let's look at this thing rationally." Dr. Ken said bending down to eye level with the upset child.

"Hmmph." KJ replied with a scowl.

"Oh no, she could save you, your brother, or your mother's life. She's slightly blue because she gets just enough oxygen to live and her habitat is cooled to reduce and slow organ function to a bare minimum. Her organs are most likely to be compatible with yours." The Dad said, slightly befuddled.

"I don't want nuthin' you stole from my Mama." The child said petulantly.

Dr. Ken smiled, "It was a painless procedure. She was inebriated as usual. I only took what I needed to create a duplicate for harvest purposes. This is a GOOD thing. Trust me."

KJ was skeptical, "I don't know Daddy. Can she ever get out and walk around?" he challenged.

"Why should she? That is not her purpose. She is like a fire extinguisher, and is only to be used during emergencies." the doctor retorted.

"I'm gonna let her out!" the little one said, with his eyes narrowing.

"Then you could be a murderer, because someone in this family could die without her use. You see, there won't be enough copies of everybody to save people with for a long time. Do you know who your closest relative is?" Dr. Ken said trying to cool the kid off.

"Abe? What does that have to do with anything?"

"No, not your brother."

"You? They name us after you."

"Your mother is your closest relative. The family name is mine, but you actually lived inside your mother for a while, until you were strong enough to come into the world."

"Yuck. Like an alien?" the kid said, incredulously.

"Only in works of fiction KJ, but amniotic fluid gave me the idea for the perfect storage medium for our mother pods for no bed-sores. I chemically created a similar solution that is constantly filtered so she can urinate and excrete. She can feed intravenously, breathe through her respirator, and remain in suspended animation for times indefinite. I call her Beta. She may be more useful than your mother ever has been." He sneered at his own remark.

Beta's wide open lifeless eyes were in Kayne's dreams this night, as he restlessly tossed and turned on his hard and cold metal cot in his cage. He awoke and found an anonymous letter that removed all doubt about the identity of his savior.

"I will wash your laundry. You have loads upon loads of it. The dirty blood money that you patronize this family business with will improve, or save lives. You can't spend it or take it with you anyway. Let it be put to a higher purpose. You may redeem lives that you have taken, or destroyed. That which is dark may be made light. A owns the day, K owns the night. I will see to it that Rent doesn't steal T-Down in your absence to ensure future revenue and profits. It would appear that you have selected a loyal descendant of Aztec warriors to be your lieutenant. They knew about sacrifice, taking no prisoners, and loyalty to the death. Tay's only request so far is your approval and access to supplemental stores of subsonic ammo for quiet and greater kill power. Message me through Doc Siskel. That is all."—X

"So Doc knew this bitch was alive all this time?! I shoulda known that old fag Jew would do anything for Pop, pining away for his ass. That muh-fucka is gonna get it too." Then he paused his exercise to mimic a televangelist preacher voice: "Yaayyeess-HUH! Oh, how the mighty have fallen! Hahaha...money-laundering hypocrites. HUH! All this bullshit to steal my fuckin money for his Frankenstein shit. Same old muh-fucka. HUH! He's like a damned cat that tortures and plays with its prey before it eats 'em." Kayne thought to himself, while doing pushups in his cell.

No one had ever believed the bizarre things he had said about his father. Everybody thought he was delusional when he opined that his father faked his own death, or that the man could actually create people and hybrid monsters.

Kayne believed Dr. Ken was capable of anything, especially after actually spending time with his obsessive yet quietly calculating father. There had been a period of connection between the two. KJ had tried to obediently please his father for a while when his Dad had made his pitch to get Kayne started in what he planned to be the family business. Everything was a means to an end with that man.

Kayne remembered the indoctrination sessions, studying and deconstructing the literature of Niccolo Machiavelli, Sun Tzu, W.E.B. DuBois, and Friedrich Nietzche, among others, under his father's intense tutelage. This brief closeness ended when KJ decided to tell his father that he was evil.

Meanwhile, the good doctor had seen to it that his little brother Abe was a devout churchgoer and steeped in biblical instruction. Poor Mama Bette had been constantly nagged to take Abe to church, probably so she could be made to squirm for her sins that week. Kayne had never taken her seriously because he found her weak and sort of funny. Lions don't usually respect antelope.

"Why those two hooked up and stayed together, I will never know. Then again, maybe I do. Kayne snickered to himself, switching to sit-

up crunches. For all her faults, Mama was dedi-
cated to us, ha!" he grunted.

Kayne had loved football. He liked the
straight-forwardness of it. Advance, score,
defend, and disrupt. He was a natural field marshal on offense at quarterback, and enjoyed
inflicting pain on defense at linebacker. Where
else could he be cheered for cracking opponents'
ribs? KJ didn't get to play for long because he
dropped out of school at 15. He played rough
street basketball in the hood on his own, with the
kind of black boys and men his father detested, in
addition to playing chess against bums, the
insane, hustlers, and ex-cons of every description,
in the municipal park downtown.

Abe, on the other hand, enjoyed the intricacies
of soccer, was a member of his student govern-
ment, chess team, debate team, Air Force ROTC,
found networking opportunities in golf, steeped
in social graces, church youth activities, and took
etiquette classes.

The Jackson boys were opponents designed to
stalemate, unless aided by an outside party to tip
the advantage one way or the other.

In retrospect, Kayne was sure that they had been prepped to play a part in his father's designs from opposite sides of the board. Dr. Ken had always enjoyed playing against himself on a cherry-wood and marble chess-table, with magnificent bronze pieces, that he kept in the far corner of his lab near his desk. He had made one move per day before starting his work, and games could go on for months.

"I know who the fuckin' bronze pieces are now muhfucka! I hope you're fuckin' amused. HUH!" Kayne grunted between pushups.

30

NOVELLA: SHADOW OF A DOUBT #10: SINS OF THE FATHER A.K.A. BETA'S MOTHER

Bette was alone. She was depressed, but glad she didn't need to sneak to smoke her cigarettes.

"What happened to all of my dreams?" she asked herself. "I sit here imagining what could've been, and I'm damn near an old hag now. Why in the name of God? I was pretty. I had so many fine men to choose from. What the hell was I thinking marrying that icicle of a man with those cold hands? That piece of shit!" she took a long drag off of one of her Virginia Slims, exhaled and tilted her glassy-eyed stare upwards to dazedly watch the smoke waft meanderingly upwards to the weathered copper and dark-stained wood Casablanca-style ceiling fan slowly spinning in her tropical plant filled living-room. She often talked to her plants. She swore it made them grow.

She was watching a TV talk-show host give paternity test results to a bunch of violent and vehemently argumentative guests:

"Okay Tyrone, according to the 99.6% accurate test results, you ARE the father!" the host proclaimed.

"Oh heyellz nawww!" the guest of honor responded.

Pandemonium onstage ensues.

Bette's friends had careers. She had been more talented than most of them in college. Yet here she reclined, wasting away this day. Most of her friends didn't show up unless it was poker night or if there was a little party going on. So she threw little dinner parties and soirees regularly. Bette's friends sampled wines that she had collected or discovered. Some even brought different varieties to try. Bette was a great cook, especially in Moroccan dishes and Spanish paellas. Her nights were lively, but her days were lonely.

The boys were off at school. Doc Siskel would occasionally go shopping with her and dish the latest dirt from the hospital and the country club, but most of the time he was pretty busy with patients. Her husband was consumed with his work, and seemed irritated by her when he was around.

Mrs. Jackson lay back down on her plush leather sofa. She raised a tumbler full of Crown in salute with a shaky hand.

"God bless ya KJ. Lord knows I try to raise ya right, you little shit. Salute." Then she downed the drink in one sloshing gulp.

"WHOOOH!" she exclaimed, squeezing her eyes shut and pounding the glass back down on living-room table. Her chest burned and she felt heat in her esophagus.

One tidbit that Doc had accidentally let slip bothered her.

"So that bastard's been cheatin' on me all this time and giving me shit whenever I slip up with somebody who actually gives a damn about me. I see. Uh-huh. I oughta kill his ass." She seethed with her eyes flashing a murderous gleam, as she steadily poured herself another drink.

The phone rang. She looked at the caller's listing.

"Speak of the Devil! Hello sonuvabitch!" she purred.

"Now honey, calm down. Things are not what they appear." Dr. Ken intoned calmly with a sigh.

"Some hooker from Mexico is LIVING in your laboratory. What the fuck am I supposed to think? I'm surprised your clammy ass can even get it up! You're a cold fish with me! If it wasn't for the boys I would've left your black ass a long time ago! I'm leaving you and I hope you catch some kinda disease that kills your ass before I do!" Bette yelled.

"I just need her to complete my implantation study. It's not what you think. What exactly did Doc tell you?" Ken said, sounding exasperated.

"Does it matter? All I know is that you've got some whore at your lab. What else could you possibly want with her? Whatever you do, don't attempt to climb your narrow ass into bed with me! You lie down with dogs, you wake up with fleas you bastard!"

"You're drinking aren't you? TYPICAL. I can't reason with a drunk. Let's just say that in order for my research to go forward, I needed a womb, for lack of a better explanation. Cloning on the cellular level is not difficult, but in order for the organism to gestate to maturity it needs a womb. Just the first one needs a human host. After that I will use the female clones to reproduce by orders of necessity. They will be genetically engineered to reach reproductive maturity quickly by the same processes that we currently use in livestock, and I will implement growth hormones commonly used in the agricultural food industry. Eva will keep quiet, and it is less risky and better than the life she had in that bordertown brothel. There is nothing to fear from her. She is making miracles possible and I thank her for her self-sacrifice. You damn sure couldn't do it. Introducing alcohol to the fetus would ruin decades of research. So I wouldn't let you do it if you wanted to." he said, smugly.

"You are one sick creep. What in the hell did I do to deserve you? I hope I didn't hear that right." she sounded like she wanted to wretch.

"Nevermind. A lush like you would never understand, much less a liberal arts major, or a poor excuse for a mother, for that matter. By the way, if you breathe a word of this to anyone, I would fear for your safety. There are some big players involved. Remember where we used to live, and look at where we live now. That should tell you something, if you were the least bit perceptive." Ken said in a calculating manner.

"Fuck You." Bette hissed.

"You could always leave you know, but this is the best place for the boys. You don't seem to mind living in the lap of luxury. This is what it takes. It's not always pleasant. Let's see how far your fake friends, that art and music foolishness takes you. The least you could do is be thankful." Dr. Ken said, with no emotion.

"I hate you." Bette hissed.

CLICK

31

NOVELLA: SHADOW OF A DOUBT #11: GENETIC WEAPONIZATION

Kayne had a visitor. Strings had been pulled to orchestrate this meeting. Doc Siskel took a seat on his side of the glass and picked up the phone. He was face to face with one Kayne Johnson, formerly Ken Jackson III, for the first time in over a decade.

Kayne slowly picked up the phone on his side of the glass. The desperate and disillusioned little boy Doc knew, was long gone. A watchful, muscular, battle-scarred, big cat of a man who

looked ready to pounce was there in his stead.
Doc was appreciative of the wire mesh and thick
glass separating them.

"This a straight-up shakedown Doc. It don't
even seem like the old man's style. I can't believe
that muhfucka has the nerve to try to get at me. I
ain't even gonna trip on the bullshit you pulled,
Doc. You dead to me now though, believe that.
You had me fooled. Ya game was tight. I
actually believed yo sucka ass thought he was
dead. Lookin' all pained at his funeral. Did
Mama know? Shit tore her up! I don't even
know why. You sat there and watched her fuckin
fall apart. Playin' the role for Pops. Why in the
hell do you do everything he says Doc? What are
you, his Stepinfetchit? His Sherpa? His Errand
boy? His Bitch? Tell his punkass this! No fuckin
deal, and you best believe I'm head-huntin any
trick tryin ta take my scratch." Kayne said, with a
fixed gaze.

"But Tay said uhh...he said uh...the deal was
a go." Doc Siskel stammered, fidgeting with the
phone.

"Wait a minute. What did you say? Who?!
This is MY shit. I don't give a fuck what Tay say.

Did you really talk to Tay? You slipping and don't even know it. One more question, mon consigliere. Why won't the old knucklehead deal with me directly? If that old rat wants this cheese he better bring his beady-eyed meddling ass out of his hole and holla at a nigga face to face, if we gonna break bread. Bet that." Kayne with finality.

"I can't guarantee that KJ. You know how he is. He wants things done in a particular order and a certain discreet way." Doc said looking evasively at his wrists.

"I've got a new name for you! Igor! HAHA-haaha, yes master, hahaha, you fuckin minion! I can't believe this shit. Dayumm! What's in it for you? Lemme ask you something. You ever seen Tay Rent? Think real carefully about how you answer. I'll know. You've lied to me all these years and I don't think I can take much more. You KILL me." Kayne asked, licking his lips, and cutting his eyes sideways at Doc, focused on him for his response.

Doc sensed the danger of his ploy.

"Where did I go wrong?" he wondered to himself. He decided to put on a brave face.

"That's not important. What matters is keeping your organization intact. Your benefactor needs money plain and simple. Without it, all his research ceases and soon. He said feigning confidence and business-like authority, he decided not to try to skim any loot off Kayne." Siskel said with certainty.

"Good. I want his work stopped. I guess that ends our meeting! HAHAHAHHA! See ya suckah! Those dreams you always used to tell me I had weren't dreams Doc. They were memories coming to me in my sleep. You acted so concerned about my mental state and my dreams. I wonder how far along that old bastard is now. Shit. He had clones when I was little What the hell does he have now?" Kayne asked.

"One could say he has diversified his portfolio of marketable defense assets. The military's loss of enthusiasm caused Dr. Ken to sweeten the pot for them in a manner of speaking. The assets have been weaponized, and accessorized." Doc said steepling his fingers.

"I don't even wanna know. It has gotta be some satanic shit. Tell me anyway. I'm listening. How can you sit there like his fuckin puppet?

Are you even listening to yourself?" Kayne asked Doc, with a smirk.

Doc Siskel's eyes took on the glazed stare of a zealot, "You can be a billionaire Kayne. Just cooperate with your father. Imagine the market-ability of a future with an all volunteer army and defense force that doesn't negatively impact even one mother back home in the good ol' USA. No political repercussions to sending clones into battle. We can be as aggressive as a superpower needs to be to keep the world in balance, and offset the population disparity with up and coming powers like China and India. These clones won't question orders, and you and your family would get a royalty cut for each and every one produced. Your money could change the world. If you don't jump on this opportunity, be advised that D.A.R.P.A. is starting to get inter-ested in funding the new assets. Then you get nothing, and get to spend the rest of your days in wild, wonderful, Utah correctional facilities. This is the place! Your father would very much prefer to keep the bloodline strong and in control of these creations and assets. Your freedom may be in the offing."

Kayne just sat looking at Doc like he had never seen him before. Even he was amazed at the level of indoctrination that Siskel had espoused. The man was finally revealed as his father's most faithful disciple.

"I'm not really surprised clones would be in combat boots Doc. What the hell are the accessories?" Kayne asked, looking mystified.

"They started out as side projects. They will make unstoppable offensive night operation teammates. I anticipated your interest. I brought you something. She is a bit of a peace offering. Your Dad remembers how much you used to love animals." Doc said, producing what looked like a small reddish-brown and black striped pit bull pup. He held it up in the palm of his hand, to the glass for Kayne to inspect it more closely.

Doc stroked the tiny pup with his finger. Kayne's eyes widened and he fogged up the glass like a little kid, as she shivered a bit and flexed a proportionate pair of fox-bat wings that had been tucked neatly under her where her forelimbs should have been.

"Awwww shit! Dayyuummm! Can I keep it?" Kayne asked, with his face pressed to the glass.

32

NOVELLA: SHADOW OF A DOUBT #12: A STAR COLLAPSES

"What the hell happened to us? Remember when we were rebellious and young? We were gonna change the world and the established order, and now we're middle-aged or old depending on who you ask, and working to keep the status quo. I should've been an artist or at least an acoustic musician, but I'm a freaking Suzy Homemaker for Chrissake. Ken is a damned nutjob gnome. You bet A mind IS a terrible thing to waste. Thanks a lot for that psycho, United Negro College Fund.

Tuskegee to the U of U. I wish he had STAYED at Tuskegee so I never would've met him! Best of all, Mr. we're here, we're queer, get used to it, gay activist Doc is STILL sneaking around in the closet after all these years! What the fuck?" Bette confided in Jose tearfully.

Spoken like a true child of the sixties, ya'll were something though. You were like your own little version of the Mod Squad. You were prettier than Peggy Lipton though. You were one vixen of a senorita." Jose whispered smoothly, in his honey-toned accent. Bette could see her reflection in his cool gaze.

"Oh so I'm a foxy lady now? Ha! Your pickup lines are pretty old too, but I like you anyway Jose. You're always here for me. Newer and fancier guys like you are after my heart, but you are still my little Latin lover before all others." Bette giggled almost to herself as she caressed Jose's angled features affectionately.

"I exist only, to put a smile on your face and to make you forget about your troubles mi amor. Forgive me if I whisper crazy things in your ear from time to time, but I love the crazy life my

sweet. Would you care for some lime or salt?"
Jose asked her.

"You like fighting too, you silly bad boy. I'm so
depressed mi amigo. I think I broke Mom and
Dad's heart for no reason all those years ago.
They were probably right after all. I just couldn't
see it. I can say I lived an interesting life by
choice, but I wonder what would've happened if I
had listened to them and just kept the faith and
married myself a good Mormon boy and just did
what I was told. Homogenized, but so what? I
ended up doing what I was told by Dr. Megalomaniac anyway. So I got myself a black jerk
instead of a white one. WOOHOO! SCORE!"
Bette exclaimed gesturing wildly with her paring
knife that she had used to slice some lime wedges
for Jose.

"Forget your heartbreak and partake of my fire
my love. I am here with you. Freak my soul with
ice cubes, and tease me with your lips and
tongue." Jose tempted her, rising to meet her lips.
She could see that she had stirred something in
him.

"My heart is breaking thinking of their disap-
pointment with me. I was their little superstar in

our stake. I could sing, dance, strum, and draw. Hell, I was almost like a little Osmond. Oops, that made me kind of sick. I feel weak." Hold me Jose. She held him close and swallowed him hungrily with her lips. Bette felt her face flush and a tingling burning sensation spreading throughout her body from the point of their last kiss.

Then, there was an unfamiliar creeping numbness beginning in her extremities as she began to swoon.

"Ooooohhh...did I uhhh? Damn you Jose! Haha...Suhhh—- sorry boys, I tried— so forgetfulll...hehe—*hiccup*— hmmm."

She vaguely remembered that she had taken too many sleeping pills before she had consumed that fateful bottle of Cuervo as she descended into dimly lit dreams of what she could've been with a smile on her face.

The iced chunky crystal tumbler slipped from her grasp as her extended arm drooped off the edge of the couch. Some ice spilled onto the carpet, but all of the tequila was gone.

Her tropical plants weren't the only quiet friends that Bette confided in and assigned personalities in her loneliness. Jose Cuervo, had been her buddy since she had been old enough to drink in Utah. She imagined him as a Benicio Del Toro type.

"Mama? Mom?! Oh Mama please! Oh, I'm so sorry I wasn't here for you Mama." Abe said, attempting to wake her when he arrived home from his BETA club meeting after school late in his senior year at high school. He had roused her from stupors before, but this time she was cool to his touch and not breathing.

Bette looked like she was sleeping peacefully on her favorite money-green leather sofa, amidst her tropical plants in the living room. She had always said green was the color of life. She wore her favorite Peruvian Alpaca sweater and wool-knit slipper socks, but she looked pale and cold.

The TV was on. One of her favorite talk-show hosts gave his final thoughts on what lessons could be learned from this episode's cast of reality characters that had spilled their guts on their deeds, cursed one another out, and fought with chairs as weapons as they tried to figure out who had impregnated whom.

Abe felt like he had left her alone too much with all his extra-curricular activities at school.

He actually looked at her prescription sleeping pill bottles and the empty tequila decanter as he called 911, so he could give the operator details for the first responders. Abe had usually ignored the paraphernalia of his mother's addictions.

The pills had been prescribed by Dr. Abraham Siskel. Abe didn't blame him. If Bette couldn't have got her pills from Doc, she would have simply got them from somewhere else. She would stay up for days at a time if she didn't have them.

"Nervous energy." She had always said.

It was at this moment that Abe decided to go into politics. He wanted to legislate for people like his Mom, who had never really stuck up for herself with actions, despite all her theatrics and threats. Maybe he could help them by telling them what to do, or their oppressors.

Bette had tried to be a good soldier. She coped by drinking and medicating herself to death, instead of leaving the man and his progeny who robbed her of her shot at life. Bette just wouldn't give up. She had always been stubborn to the point of self-detriment.

In the end she had subjugated all her desires and aspirations to her unloving husband, and to her kids. One of whom, KJIII, was a criminal, seemed to regard her as unworthy of anything but disrespect for allying herself with the father he hated. The other, Abe himself, made less and less time for his former best friend as he became increasingly wrapped up in his own pursuits in life.

Bette left her life the way she lived it: Unfulfilled.

There was one exception. One person truly made her feel like she had accomplished something of which she could be proud.

Abe knelt next to her reclining figure on the couch, and kissed her lifeless but smiling face on the forehead, while squeezing her petite, ornately nail-polished and manicured hand.

"I love you Mama. Typical of you, smiling through the pain, to the very end."

33

NOVELLA: SHADOW OF A DOUBT #13: A REVELATION

Security cameras at the Mallmart were busy on Black Friday. Shoppers were in a frenzy. An observer through the one-way security glass could see a trio of teen to twenty-somethings strolling around in black waterproof hooded parkas, with extra long grey tee-shirts, work-boots and oversize jeans.

Local cops would have recognized a clique of T-downers were in the building, like a small pack of wolves among the holiday sheep, who were a bit carnivorous themselves this day. The clique seemed a bit uncomfortable in the glaring lights and domestic cultural submersion.

Oddly enough, the smallest one of the crew who was pushing the cart seemed to be directing the others in selecting items for purchases. The little one was about 5'3 wearing shades and toboggan black knit hat, and seemed to be a chatterbox who gestured constantly and just couldn't seem to keep still. The loudest, bossiest, and most memorable one of bunch was the least identifiable except as the only one without facial hair.

Tejas Renteria was shopping. It was a bizarre Christmas list.

"Ziploc baggies, check. Drano, check. Vaseline, check. Styrofoam cups, check. Five-gallon gasoline container, check. Gasoline, check after we get to the pump. Ajax cleaner, check. Electrical tape, check. Duct tape, check. Wool socks, check. Pipe cleaners, check. Butane lighters, check. Rubber gloves, check. Nails, check. Pay-as-you-go phone, check. We can get things popping for under seventy-five dollars and one-stop shopping. Boom boom boom boom! Bang bang bang bang! Vamenos! Vamenos! Hahahaha!"

Tay exclaimed excitedly. Was this Christmas spirit?

"Are we done yet Tay. Can we get outta here now?" one of the T-downers asked, moping almost comically.

"Yeah, you two. I guess that's the list. We gotta split up and buy this shit seperately. You can do so much with a little dinero and an attitude. We about to set this shit off if that muthafucka renigs on his deal to get Kayne out. Get me a team of street-soldiers together for this meeting with whats-his-name?" Tay said, looking like she was trying to remember.

"Doc Siskel, you know, Kayne's friend. We don't need nobody for him." one of the Tees responded.

"So what? Nobody's catching me slipping either. I got a lot of shit on my mind, this is hectic. If he was really Kayne's friend he wouldn't be shaking us down, this favor would be free. Running this shit is a headache. I'm getting candy Kayne back to run his candy shop, dammit. We're going in four deep to show him its real and he betta be straight. Let's go now. Haha, well you get to go through the checkout line Stevie. I'll be in the car. That's what happens when you whine like a little vato. My advice is the self-checkout. C'mon Tyson, you with me! Stevie you take the cart." Tay commanded and sent the shopping cart careening towards Stevie with a mischievous chuckle, almost mowing down shoppers in the process.

"Naaawwww. Tay! C'mon. Tay! Ty! Stop playin! Stevie yelled as Tay chucked a small rubber-banded roll of cash towards him and ran out of the store laughing hysterically, with Tyson following close behind, grinning and giving Stevie double middle fingers on the way out the sliding glass doors.

The white-haired greeter who was stationed next to the entrance/exit looked horrified and taken aback.

"Damned gangbangers." She fumed. "Can't even get ready for Christmas in peace."

Doc Siskel had arrived at Kayne's downtown operations center. The building had seen better days. Its busted windows, crumbling red brick walls and peeling paint said it was abandoned. The intermittent stream of visitors coming and going through the front door said otherwise.

Police cruisers drove by every thirty minutes seemingly oblivious to what was hidden in plain sight. Doc parked in a vacant lot across the street so that he could see if his vehicle was approached from any direction, and awaited his phone call from Tay Rent.

This was the moment he had been waiting for. Doc had always wanted to get in on something big early. Military contracts had been lucrative but had too many strings attached and budgetary oversight on Dr. Ken's research. If he could bring the Jackson heir back into the fold the monetary resources would be unrestricted. Criminal enterprises care only about profit, not where the money comes from. He had hung close to Dr. Ken because he had always believed that some of that man's projects would be killer apps and make him and his family billionaires, and hopefully his most loyal friend, counselor, and initial investor: Doc Siskel himself.

He had a contract drawn up with Dr. Ken that entitled him to 33% stake of all profits from successful projects and patents in exchange for getting money from his trust fund when they were both fresh out of college and Jackson needed seed money to buy equipment and supplies to begin his research. Doc had also done everything he could to ensure that Dr. Ken would be able to focus wholly on his work, and gave him money when he was between contracts and grants. He had damn near raised his kids for him, and had tried to prep KJIII for a leadership role as patriarchal heir to the fortune that he was sure would come.

A text from Tay lit up and vibrated his cell phone on the dashboard of his Saab.

"Showtime." Siskel muttered.

Doc Siskel got out of his car and gripped the silver knob on his walking stick tightly as he briskly crossed the street and went up the front stairs to a splintering pair of wooden doors at the main entrance. The doors swung open and Doc entered and found himself face to face with four T-downers who were holding the weapons of their choice. They were standing on a landing between the first floor and the basement, with steps trailing up and down behind them.

"Well don't just stand there old man. Tay waitin' on you." One of the Tees said.

Doc entered and headed up to the first floor with two escorts in front of him and two behind him. When they topped the stairs they went down a dark hall and into a room where a short, olive-skinned, dark-eyed host welcomed him and motioned for him to sit down and talk business.

"You got a way to get him out of a supermax prison Doc?" an unfamiliar voice asked.

"What is all this?" Doc asked looking at a table full of homemade bombs.

"He told me he is willing to cut you in, but don't think of crossing us. I know he knows you, but I don't know you, and I don't like you nibbling at our cheese, vato." Tay Rent hissed. Doc thought the little capo was dangerously beautiful. He had never seen such long dark eyelashes on a man, and he had loved many pretty men.

"I don't know what you're planning on doing with this stuff, but we can get him out thanks to a backroom deal from the Governor. It's practically done, if we come together." Doc bluffed, eyeing Tejas nervously. He was captivated by Renteria's striking features and youthful appearance and intimidating presence despite a diminutive size.

The small face was intently focused on him.

Then it struck him. He knew why Kayne had known he hadn't met with Tejas Renteria before now.

"I want him back." Tay said rising as Doc sat down. Renteria pulled the knit ski hat off, and jet black hair flowed down past her shoulders. K-A-Y-N-E was tattooed across her right hand's knuckles, and a barbed wire ring was tattooed on her left hand's ring finger.

"I want my Kandy Kayne, and if you try to fuck my man over, one of these is going up your ass, then we are gonna start blowing up everyone and everything you have ever loved." The little queen bee said with a sweeping gesture towards the improvised explosives.

"Comprende?" she asked, and smiled sweetly.

34

NOVELLA: SHADOW OF A DOUBT #14: BATTLE PREPARATIONS

"First of all, I would like to thank ya'll for coming out in this cold, pig-slaughtering weather to see me tonight. Early cold snap, huh? HaHa! I sure appreciate ya! Thank you for your support. Ya'll simmer down now. Simmer down. Hehheh. Thank ya. I just wanna say a few things that a lot of ya'll are thinking, but are too polite and genteel to say. Seems our southern hospitality has gotten the better of us. There's a scallawag in the Governor's mansion." a short man with graying, straw-colored hair proclaimed from step-stool hidden behind a podium.

"My opponent is soft on crime. He let a drug-dealin, gun-runnin, murderer go on living on the backs of taxpayers. Do you know how many thousands of dollars a year it takes to house, feed, clothe, secure, guard, and medically treat a maximum security inmate? It's higher than the average FAMILY income in our commonwealth. How could anybody grant a stay of execution for scum like Kayne Johnson, and claim to want to clean up our communities?" the candidate asked, hitting his stride.

"He might as well lay out a welcome mat for criminals who prey on good god-fearing folk in our great state. What kills me about it is that this same charlatan is pro-abortion. What? Is it wrong to put to death those who had a chance at a productive life, but chose to terrorize and kill our citizens, and at the same time condone not even giving the innocent unborn a chance at life? I say NO! It's time to take this country back from a bunch of slimy, double-dealing, limp-wristed lawyers, like Abe Jackson. I say let's return to some good ol' common sense." Clint said, gaining confidence from the crowd.

"I ain't no purtyboy. I ain't got a whole bunch of fancy degrees on my wall. I got one from Virginia Military Institute, and that was enough to make my Ma and Pa proud. Common sense is what we need in this commonwealth. I came up on a farm. You get up at the crack of dawn and you work till the cows come home. I'm from the Bible belt and I say we need to get back to both." Webber said with a toothy smile, to "whoops" of support from the audience.

"You got these citified smooth-talkers like Abe Jackson trying to take our guns away, but criminals like Kayne Johnson don't have any trouble gettin' guns. Kayne Johnson's gang is a para-military operation, plain and simple. Hell, he bartered guns for drugs with Mexican rebels and cartels, and then brings that poison on home to us. With the amount of drugs his boys got him busted with, the amount of weapons traded must've been enough to take Iwo Jima."

"Kill him!" a voice from the crowd shouted. C.W. waved him off with a laugh.

"I was a soldier and a cop before I started my own business. I know what to do with these dirt-bags. I will keep your families safe. I will clean up our streets. I ain't scared to get my hands dirty. I ain't scared to roll up my sleeves and work hard for ya'll. I believe in God. I believe marriage is between a man and a woman. I am pro-life. I believe gun-control is having the good gun owners in control. No more handouts. You don't work, you don't eat. Abe Jackson and his cronies are taxing us to death so they can take care of a bunch of shiftless freeloaders!" C.W. said pumping his fist.

"My name is Clint Webber, ya'll can call me C.W., and I would be proud to take your voice and your values to the national stage in our Senate. Let's take this country back to greatness. That Jackson has done enough damage as our governor. The last thing Virginia needs is him in our nation's Senate making us look like fools. He doesn't deserve to bear the surname of Old Hickory Andrew, or the great general, Stonewall. I'll do ya proud! HaHa! Wooh!"

Thunderous applause.

"I'll tell ya'll something else. I say that Jackson has been a disgrace and is criminal for saving Johnson. I say the two are peas in a pod, as my Ma used to say. Hell, they even look alike if you ask me. Pa used to say if walks like a duck, shoot it, it's good eatin, nah, you know how the rest was supposed to go! Hahaha! I'm just messing. Good night ya'll! Don't forget to vote Clint Webber for Senator in November! See you on the campaign trail. Spread the word. Talk to your friends and neighbors. We need ya! God bless!" Clint waved to the crowds that had come out to see Lexington's favorite son at the outdoor amphitheatre despite the drizzle and cold.

The crowd was fired up.

As C.W. departed the stage, he made a big motion with his hands like Moses parting the Red Sea, and then navy blue stage curtains that had been draped behind him divided to reveal a 30-foot billboard with Abe and Kayne's heads depicted as peas in a big green peapod with the slogan underneath: Get rid of these peas in a pod, vote for Clint, common sense, and bring back God!

The crowd went beserk. They were waving their cell-phones and yelling, hooting, and hollering like they were at a rock concert. A few rebel yells and screams pierced the night air like echoes of the past. Supporters jumped up and down partly to keep warm, but mostly out of excitement about their fiesty little candidate. C.W. was a short guy, but he was a ruddy, blue-eyed, square-jawed, fireplug of a man who could handle himself in a brawl, and win over a crowd that had gathered to watch.

Governor Abe Jackson had watched a broadcast of the performance of his upcoming rival with his spin doctors, campaign manager, political gurus, and a few aides. They had laughed off and joked about much of C.W.s speech, but they were kind of quiet by the end of it. Abe looked around the room coolly, but masked his concern that they were all looking at him as if they were seeing him for the first time. He decided to go on the offensive to keep their minds from wandering into places he didn't want them thinking about.

"Why am I not surprised this little redneck would say we all look alike!" Abe bluffed. "We gotta hit back! I need ideas people. I am categorically opposed to the death penalty and we've fought these battles before. What I need is a response that I can beat this guy's tough talk with. What can I do with deathrow inmates that would be redemptive or spinnable as a way to use the finality of death against this little dipshit hayseed. I want you thinking out of the box people. I already am. When we debate I am going to destroy this prick. I'm gonna wipe the floor with him and smile the whole time. Whatcha got? Just throw stuff at me." Abe asked expectantly.

"Sir you have a call waiting on line 9." a staffer interjected.

Abe grabbed the phone. "Got it. This had better be important."

"Hey Abe. Did you see what I saw?" Doc Siskel asked.

Abe sighed, "Yeah, we're game-planning for this guy as we speak. Why didn't you just call my cell? Did you have something important to tell me about? We kind of have a fire to put out here."

"This is more dramatic my boy. I have a solution. Sometimes being old has its benefits, though they are few." Doc chuckled. He was

absolutely relieved when he had seen the broadcast. He was puffing one of his beloved Sancho
Panzas, and sipping Cognac in celebration of his
deliverance from the beautiful terror that was
Tay Rent.

"Really?" Abe asked hopefully. He was like a
man who was ready to beat the crap out of somebody with anything he could find within arm's
reach.

"You ever seen The Dirty Dozen?" Doc asked
with a laugh and an obvious swig from his goblet,
that could be heard over the phone.

"Are you drunk? What the hell are you talking
about? I gotta go Doc." Abe said kind of pissed.

"You know they used to put the worst of the
worst on the front lines and high-risk operations
in battle, my boy. How's that strike you? HAHA-
HAHA! We will hit this joker from the right. He
will never see it coming." Doc was downright
giddy.

"But then Kayne would be like free." Abe said.

"Mine fodder, but yes. He would." Doc said
and laughed, drank, and puffed some more. "But
you could spin him from parasitic predator, to

gladiator for the cause. I'm sure you could sell it."

"What am I paying all these guys for? I think I need to drink what you've been drinking." Abe said smiling, and ready to go to war.

"Well, you aren't paying half of them, but it is GOOD STUFF. Heehee!" Doc responded, and it sounded like he dropped the phone.

35

NOVELLA: SHADOW OF A DOUBT #15: DENIABILITY

"Do not let your left hand know what your right hand is doing.— Matt 6:3 New King James Version" C.W. intoned the verse aloud as he stared intently at his monitor perusing web-based info on his opponent's public record.

He and his staffers and aides hadn't succeeded in finding much mud to sling at the Governor who would be Senator Abe Jackson. Abe was not an outstanding politician, but he blended in with the rest of the mediocrity in political circles pretty well. Camoflauged. One thing intrigued Clint though.

"Ain't it kinda odd how all his family members just have sorta disappeared?" C.W. said squinting and scratching his head with ruddy and stubby fingers.

"I mean it's like all the political liabilities that lived under that one roof with him have been peeled away from him like rotten banana-skins leaving him clean as a whistle. Maybe this ain't no coincidence. I mean his Mom was a hippie who seems to have ended up a raging alcoholic. His brother seems to have gone off the radar and is thought to be dead from a drugdeal gone bad. His daddy was up to his eyeballs in something for both the military and the healthcare uppity ups and died awhile back but something seems fishy about it cause the appropriations from the budget for his research are STILL coming out according to a little birdie I know, it seems to have gone from public to classified for national security. Pretty unethical stuff from what I gather. I gotta find a way to get AT HIM." Clint said through clenched teeth.

"We should put a private investigator on this.
You need to be campaigning 24/7 and raising
money to beat the band. You need to be out front
selling the dream to the people. Its almost like
you are running against an incumbent. Keep jab-
bing at him with the Kayne Johnson pardon and
the soft on crime front. Fear sells. We got to get
his potential sponsors and donors nervous about
him. You have to be the white knight. This guy
came from weirdos and garbage. You have to be
the man to clean it up. Thats what we're selling."
his campaign manager, Rex Firebaugh, advised
him.

"I got an aunt down in Texas who was a cop
for over twenty years. Those ungrateful bastards
laid her off just a few years before she was due for
retirement. She's got a nose like a bluetick
hound. She is sharp as a tack and a bit down on
her luck here lately. Her intuition was a little too
good. She busted her husband of twenty years
screwing around on her. Bigdaddy Schaeffer was
some dirtbag truckdriver with a girlfriend in
every state in the Gulf Coast." C.W. said thought-
fully.

"If she is so sharp, why didn't she catch that old fool earlier?" Rex snickered.

"According to her, she paid him no mind because she trusted him. Once she lost her job she had nothing better to do than snoop on him. This might do her some good and keep her busy. I'd like to keep it in the family and give my aunt Hannah a little project. She'll sure as shootin need the distraction. I'll give her a call. Two birds with one stone. Yeah boy." C.W. said gaining confidence.

"Sounds like a plan. We need somebody good at digging up dirt. I hope you are her favorite nephew." Rex agreed nodding and rubbing his meaty palms together.

36

NOVELLA: SHADOW OF A DOUBT #16: LOVE CHILD LOST

"I guess this is goodbye Haysoose. You pretty much changed my opinion of colo… I mean afro-ameri… I mean umm… what DO YOU call yourself?" Hannah chuckled, clasping her hands, and batting her fake lashes at him sweetly.

"I'm just black… and mexican. you don't have a problem being called white. That always cracks me up when you start tiptoeing around it. I wanted to make a good impression on you though, Hannah. You really helped me get some good experience under my belt and you pretty much told me from the jump everything that I would be up against being the new guy on the force. You are a good ol' gal. I was sorry to hear about what a fool ol' Bigdaddy has been to you, and how dirty they did you before you could retire from the force. I wish you the best up there in Virginia." Jesus said, shifting his weight nervously from one foot to another, looking sort of sideways at the the short, stocky, blonde belle with the bee-hive bun. Jesus occasionally had to sway to dodge the hanging flowerbaskets on Schaeffer's porch as they swung in periodic stiff breezes.

"You know I don't want to offend my favorite little hotshot whippa-snappa at the precinct. I would never say it if I didn't like ya. You're a good fella. Heck if I was a younger lily of the field you might've had the privilege of taking me out…hahahaha… ya are a little sweetheart though. Don't let those other guys giving you the crappy assignments get you down. Keep them ears perked up and those brown eyes shining. Keep plugging away at it okay? C'mere and give your old pahtnah a hug." Officer Schaeffer said reaching up with open arms, and on her tiptoes, toward the sheepish officer who towered over her uncomfortably on her front porch.

They embraced. Jesus was sort of embarassed that he was sort of turned on by her hug. She smelled like lavender and soap. He was going to miss her. She had been his little Marm in a squad car. He could tell she had been a looker back in the day, but she was thirty years his senior. Now was not the time to get overly stimulated.

"Down Boy! WTF?! Stop that! Calm down, this chick probably wears dentures man!" Jesus chided himself in a sort of disbelief.

For someone of her generation and line of work to overcome her former predjudice meant something to Jesus. He knew a disproportionate number of the perps they picked up were black or mexican. Jesus was both. He appreciated her honesty with him.

He had never trusted a woman since his mom and baby sister had disappeared almost twenty years ago. His Dad had let his mother visit him a few times, but he had always talked about her like she was a dog. Jesus knew she had struggled with addiction, and her name was Eva Moreno. She had gotten mixed up with the wrong people trying to support her habit and a baby girl.

His Dad had been stationed at Lackland Air Force Base up in San Antonio. Jesus may have been the result of a wild weekend off base and partying down in Laredo. Marcus Brown constantly told Jesus that one night a mistake could kill all his dreams and aspirations with the burden of raising a child.

Jesus suspected his parents had been together longer than his Dad admitted. Had his Dad tried to make a ho into a housewife? It might explain his father's anger and denial of his Mexican side. This iritated Chris, which was why he told everybody he met to just call him Jesus to make it sound even more Mexican, much to his father's chagrin. Marcus had a hard time not taking out his anger at Eva while trying to raise Jesus, especially when he finally married and had more favored kids with Jesus' stepmom, Sadie.

Jesus had heard whispers that Eva had been working in a brothel in Nueva Laredo on the other side of the border. His little half-sister was named Tejas. He had only seen her when she was newborn and tiny, just before Eva vanished.

Though her father was thought to be a Hispanic john, she was born in Laredo, TX in the USA. Eva wanted to leave no doubt about her citizenship, thus the name.

No other woman had ever trusted Jesus with her life like his partner, Hannah. He was a player of sorts, and this trust and bond with any woman was new to him. He was unsure how to feel about it, or how to react. Did he like Hannah as a mother figure or want to do her? Sometimes, he just didn't know.

" So what exactly are you gonna do up there in Virginia? You gonna be alright? I'll be sure to come check on you sometime. You aint never been nowhere but here." Jesus questioned her in a faltering tone, finally holding eye contact.

"Private investigation. Pretty cool huh? It's for my nephew's political campaign. He might be a Senator if the chips fall right. His Mama would be so proud. He always was a good'uhn. At least when he kept his temper. A little hot-headed but the kind that will have your back when you need him to ... sort of like a certain member of present company." Hannah replied rather pleased with herself. She had noticed with a bit of alarm that

Jesus was looking at her sort of strangely. He usually averted his eyes from her, but he was gazing at her as if transfixed.

"I want to come with you." Jesus said with resolution.

"What?!" Hannah said putting a hand to her heart. "Stop talking crazy and looking at me with that deer-in-the-headlights look. It's just nerves Haaysoose. You can make it just fine here without me around. I AM flattered, but I'm not what you need. You really are just too cute sometimes. Bless your heart. You don't need to protect me. I'm a big girl and I will take care of myself. I learned alot from you too you know." she kissed him on the cheek and chuckled, blushing.

"When are you leaving Schaeffer? I'll help you pack." Officer Brown said.

"I'm packing up the ol' Mustang first thing in the morning. I'm leaving most of my stuff. Too many memories attached to the big jerk and the stuff in this house. He can have the house as far as I am concerned. I should've left a long time ago. You be good Haysoose. Now git!" Hannah said and practically ran back inside the house.

She thought she had now officially seen it all. She felt butterflies flitting around in her stomach and she was a bit out of breath. She hadn't had that tingle in years.

"I'm gonna take a powder." she thought, and headed for the medicine cabinet.

Jesus walked slowly back to his black-and-white with his head hanging down as the south Texas sun set in fiery hues, and the wind breezed through the rural brush in front of the little yellow clapboard house with all the flower boxes and birdfeeders, on dusty County Route 9.

37

NOVELLA: SHADOW OF A DOUBT #17: PONDERINGS IN THE PIT

Dr. Ken's growing inventory was becoming a problem. His facilities were getting cramped because they were designed for researching organ regeneration and hybrid clone combinations, not warehousing and mass producing his wares after he had figured out how to make them. Either he would have to find alternative customers for his products, or he would have to cull some of them. The military gladly wiped out his male inventory, but had met it's female quotas.

He needed a hi-tech and clandestine storage facility. D.A.R.P.A had gotten wind of his accomplishments and was offering him one. He was ready to break off negotiations with his hard-headed incarcerated son, Kayne. Dr. Ken didn't need or want him or his dirty money anymore.

"Let him rot." he thought.

Dr. Ken had banished Kayne once and his latest correspondence made him feel he had been correct in making that decision.

Kayne had propositioned him with the idea to market some of the females, of which he had an overabundance, as the natural progression of lonely loser companions. If some guys were desperate enough to buy blow-up dolls and hookers, why not disease-free and unused flesh and blood female receptacles. Some would be one-time purchases for long-term use as mates, and others would be put in rotation for hourly services. Others could be used as mules to carry illicit drugs from Laredo, TX up the I-35 corridor and outward to connecting interstates, in their body cavities as mules.

Dr. Ken had messaged him back, "That kind of thinking is why you are in jail. Most of them look like your mother. Imagine them being put to such a purpose. That would debase your mother's memory."

Dr. Ken cringed to think his first-born son would think so criminally. He had attempted to mold him into what W.E.B. DuBois would have referred to as a member of the black population's "talented tenth."

Kayne's idea made business sense. Dr. Ken just didn't aspire to be a lowly pimp. He wanted to be Prometheus. The fire of the gods he had stolen was the formula to create and re-create life. He had created new breeds of animals for pragmatic applications. He had re-grown human brains, livers, kidney, and lungs.

He had cloned human life to save human life. He aspired to be a God of sorts.

Dr. Jackson felt his generation of black people worked hard as if they had to prove to America that they were just as good as their white counterparts. They were the generation of Dr. Martin Luther King, Malcolm X, and Booker T. Washington, W.E.B. DuBois before them.

Kayne's generation of blacks and those that followed it mystified him. They took everything for granted. They had never fought for the right to vote. They had never been part of the countless students staging sit-ins and boycotts of segregated institutions and businesses. The Klan didn't hunt them down. Lynchmobs were unheard of. Many killed each other of their own volition. A lot of this generation's role models thought jail equated to street cred. Slang was preferable to articulate english. Academic excellence was equated to selling out or acting white. And now this ...

"I create human clones and the first thing that comes to my son's mind is to pimp them as whores, and run drugs with them." he thought as he went about his daily feeding tasks from aisle to aisle and pen to pen. The usually unemotional man was outraged. Was some of his anger because he had considered using that miscreant's money to further his own cause when his military and governmental sponsors had seemed to hesitate?

For now, Dr. Ken was using some of his female inventory to help him maintain and care for his facility and it's occupants. It enabled him to observe their intelligence level and trainability. It had been difficult at first but as they became acclimated to their tasks his life got easier and he was able to make more time for his research projects. One special project took up most of his time these days.

His income was steady due to military applications of creations. They were literally "killer apps." As long as they weren't exposed to outside influences their obedience was unquestioning. The military loved them and kept their units segregated and secret for fear free thought would contaminate their efficiency. They didn't have to unlearn anything. They just had to be told what to do.

Dr. Ken's litters of Pit-Bats were going out the door as fast as he could produce them. Special forces loved the Hell-terriers as they called them. His mixture of species within kingdoms had been key. Pit-bull terriers and flying foxes are both mammals, thus the genetic leap hadn't been as far as trying to mix reptiles and bird for instance, or fish and amphibians, just stick to mixing mammals with dissimilar mammals, reptiles with dissimilar reptiles, and fish with dissimilar fish, etc.

Dr. Ken's latest masterstroke was in successfully harnessing the 500 watt renewable energy of electric eels crossbred with air-breathing giant amphibious snakehead fish. His hybrid fishzilla was about 4.5 feet-long and could survive in water or on land. Their shallow-water pens were strategically placed throughout his lab. Most were kept next to the most power-sapping pieces of equipment to keep them directly charged. They were guardians of the lab as well. A security breach would open hatches to their pens spilling water across the floor and potentially releasing 500 volts of fury from each of them. Their domain was the expansive floor.

The Pit-bat pens were second-tier about counter-top level off the ground lining the perimeter of the central laboratory. A security breach would open sliding doors on their cages. Their domain was the air and the dark. They mostly slept during the day, but they had a pitbull's sense of smell and bite, a bat's sonic radar and wings. There was no escaping them.

An intruder would've thought they had entered hell itself. Shortly thereafter they would find out firsthand what the afterworld holds. Both security forces were carnivorous, so disposal of the remains would be messy but discreet.

Dr. Ken used all the bio-waste that his subjects produced to fertilize a dense garden that hid within an fir tree lined wall that had enclosed a forgotten cemetery behind the old rectory. He had assigned a special caretaker to its maintenance.

She did most of her work at dusk or dawn. She was a long-term project. The caretaker had re-grown brain tissue, skin tissue, and liver tissue. She had been slow to rehabilitate. Her natural affinity for the garden had helped. She had finally begun to speak again. For years there had been understanding in her eyes but she had finally begun to express herself. Her old age was truly a second childhood. She had re-learned everything from walking to now talking.

His wife had been a blank slate when he had begun duplicating her brain cells and matter.

Dr. Ken doubted she recognized him and remembered their connection. She was his ultimate and most secret accomplishment. He had blamed himself for her brain-death and made her re-animation a part of his life's work.

Resurrection.

"Ahhhh-saaahhh. Gaahhhduhn. Da liiiiiiiyyy." she babbled.

"I'm sorry. You'll have to wait to go outside. Can you help me hanging the I.V. feed bags? You know what time it is. It's feeding time. I'll only give you the food and bags for the lower-tier and the little ones. They are low enough for you to reach. You know the drill. I will let you go into the garden when you begin enunciating better. You tend to get clearer as the evening approaches. Keep trying." Dr. Ken encouraged his aged helper.

Bette was graying and in her 60s, but the light in her eyes was that of youth still discovering the world.

She smiled at the thought and almost hopped. "Twiii—lyyyyy! Liyyyy!"

"That was pretty close. Hurry up and finish. I might even bring your paints out in the twilight." Dr. Ken coaxed. He thought he had never seen

Bette this happy in her younger days before her
overdose.

38

NOVELLA: SHADOW OF A DOUBT #18: STRATEGIC SNITCHING

It was a house of cards really. Secrets inter-locked three tiers of power from Machiavel-lian military medical science, to a high polit-ical office, to the criminal underworld and the streets. The secretive patriarch and researcher, Dr. Ken Jackson Jr. knew it. Abe Jackson, the Governor may have sensed it. Most importantly, the man who stood to gain the most from its collapse, the incarcerated Kayne, knew it.

He was ready to get out. The only thing pre-venting his freedom had been his code.

"THOU SHALT NOT SNITCH."

Kayne was beginning to think the code didn't apply unless you broke bread at the table of the dinner thieves. His Dad and his brother were square niggas, but they did dirt with no honor. They had never helped him make money. Kayne made no bones about what he was, but those two denied the selfishness of their purpose. Kayne had played along with his father and his brother's games. Now his brother, the Governor, wanted him getting shot at and used as mine-bait on the frontlines in a war he didn't give a shit about.

Kayne saw no benefit to himself in Abe's prop-osition. He only saw a man who wanted to win public office so badly that he would gladly sacri-fice his brother to make political publicity. Con-victs on the frontlines was not a new idea, but Kayne was pissed about it. He was fine with three hots, a cot, and the free healthcare he got. Hell, he could go to college in here if he wanted. He had been reading up on criminal justice lately. It was the source of his new inspiration. But being told what and when to do everything grated at his very core.

Kayne was fed up with his father too. The condescending prick had reneged on a deal to free Kayne eventually, and give him a cut of the profits and the family biz after funneling money from T-Down to fund Dr. Ken's research and development projects.

As soon as the military pounced on Dr. Ken's prototypes and initial hybrid animal offerings, he had swiftly back-pedaled away from his commitments to Kayne. The bastard had even sold the pit-bat pup that he had promised to Kayne as a peace-offering.

Kayne was having a hard time keeping his girl, Tay, from blowing up the messenger and sycophant of his fathers machinations, his old childhood confidant, Doctor Abraham Siskel.

"Calm yo ass down girl. No need for that, Tay baby. Instead of blowing up Doc Siskel, why don't we put the real muthafucka behind all this shit up on blast, and that little brother goody-goody Abe too. Remember that package you safe deposited for me on Abe a while back?" he asked her through the phone, aware that their conversation might be eavesdropped on.

"Hold up. Nigga just spose to walk around breathin and shit after I TOLD him I would kill him if they fucked us over?!" Tay huffed.

"I didn't stutter. Yeah. I hear that dude Abe is running against hired a P.I. Find out who it is and send duplicates of the DNA genealogy and paternity info I stashed. We gonna blow this shit up for real. That possum-ass frankenstein nigga playin dead is gonna come to light and when the media gets a hold to Abe after they find out he pardoned me, hahaha...his big brotha, they gonna wanna kill his ass. C'mon Tay, laugh, its gonna be funny." Kayne whispered.

"Hmph." Tay grunted.

"I left out the best part babe." Kayne said, with excitement.

"What, Kayne?" Tay asked, confused.

"Once it comes to light that I am Ken Jackson III, and not the Kayne Johnson 55-gallon barrel drumboy alias, its gonna get crazy. All the eyewitnesses who snitched on me are dead. They testified against Kayne Johnson. He was convicted of the crimes, not me! Hahaha...but he's dead already. Pretty smooth to set up a dead man as the patsy don't you think? I got one word for you."

"No shit?" Tay asked, excitedly.

"MISTRIAL." Kayne bubbled.

"Baby!?"

"I don't give a fuck if these muthafuckas can hear me! I'ma be outta this bitch soon. I remember my punkass little brother quoting scriptures and shit sayin: There is a time and place for everything! Hahahaha! IT'S TIME TO SNITCH BITCHES! HAHHAhahah! Fuck yall! All of you muthafuckas! I'ma see you outside muthafuckas! TRUST! DADDY'S COMIN' HOME BABY!" Kayne exclaimed.

Tay squealed with glee.

39

NOVELLA: SHADOW OF A DOUBT #19: RUMBLINGS

A wine-colored 1966 Ford Mustang Standard Coupe hurtles from the southern horizon up the interstate in the fast lane, with its V-8 humming a baritone tune. The driver does not sit very high in the saddle. An ash-blonde beehive bun stands out against the black interior through the shiny glass and chrome.

Most of the traffic clears out of her way. Some honk and stare. Some give her the finger. Some give her a thumbs up. Hannah doesn't stick around long enough to pay any mind to any of their reactions. Not too long ago she would've wrote somebody like herself a ticket. The loaded . 380 in her ankle-holster wouldn't have made a good impression either.

Ms. Priss sits in the front passenger seat wiggling her whiskers and looking rather calm with the exception of her twitching the tip of her silver-blue tail. Her jade-colored eyes are slightly narrowed as she looks over the dark dash through the windshield at the scenery racing to meet them. Her claws are slightly dug into the seat to keep her stationary. She is used to riding with Hannah, but it is a rare treat. She is that rare cat that enjoys a car. Most of the time her place was the small backseat, but it is filled with luggage, plants, and a picnic cooler. She is enjoying the view for a change.

Hannah's old partner, Haysoose Brown, wouldn't have been so cool. He didn't appreciate Officer Schaeffer's moon-shiner's daughter style of driving in the old Crown Vic police cruiser most of the time, but the idea of her pissed off and lead-footing it up the road in her smaller, lighter, and even more powerful baby probably would've given him heart palpitations.

Hannah smiled to think of his probable reaction. Haysoose was such an unusual rookie. He usually drove like a grandma. She wondered if she would ever see him again. She wiped away a tear. She needed a laugh. Big Daddy Schaeffer had been her high-school sweetheart. Their marriage of over 30 years had just been rent asunder by her discovery of his rampant cheating. She and her Russian cat were barreling their way towards a completely new life in Virginia.

Hannah's cell-phone started pulsating to the ring-tone of Santana's "Black Magic Woman," and her cat puffed up and jumped out of her seat with a yowl of surprise. Ms. Priss hated that thing. She had forgotten she was sitting next to it. Hannah fumbled around, and then snatched it up to her ear before Ms. Priss could pounce on it and exact her revenge.

"Hello?" she asked without checking the caller info.

"Is this Hannah Webber Private Investigations Service?" a slightly accented female voice asked.

"Ummm...yes maam, what can I do for you?" Hannah said trying to get used to being called Webber again in the near future.

"That is the question isn't it Mami?" the caller's voice giggled.

"I'm tryin' ta be polite maam, but I ain't got time for no mess! If this is a prank hang up. If not, get to the point of ya call." Hannah replied tersely, trying to watch the road and her cat sullenly reclaiming its perch. She glanced at the speedometer. She hadn't realized she was doing 103 miles per hour. Oh well, at least she wasn't applying eyeliner. She was ready to burn rubber on her past life. This new one was starting before she could even get to her destination.

"Wow. Maybe I should've gotten into this business sooner." Hannah thought.

"I have information on Governor Abe Jackson that will be a lethal weapon for your nephew's campaign for Senate. I'm sure Clint Webber would pay YOU through the nose to get it, despite being your nephew. This is some high-powered shit. The question is: What are you willing to do to get it? Huh Mami?" the voice teased and cooed.

"Is this a joke? What the hell do you mean what am I willing to do? I'll do whatever is legal and make it worth your while, but cut the shit alright?" Hannah replied, becoming increasingly exasperated with the silliness of the caller's manner. Ms. Priss could tell that Hannah was getting mad too. She was staring up at her intently with her ears pricked up.

"One of my guys will meet you and deliver the goods in a locked attache suitcase at the greyhound bus station in Lexington at 11pm tomorrow night. I expect payment in cash of only $5000 and more info you have on your nephew's involvement in a skinhead faction when he was stationed at Fort Bragg in North Cakalaka... hahaha! Don't play dumb, we already know, just a little leverage ya know Mami? Any way we want it documented and corroborated. You are a P.I. now right?" Tay asked with a cool chortle.

"He was just a knuckle-head boy back then. He ain't much of a racist, he just wanted to fit in with those guys that partied the hardest on base. He grew out of that crap. That horse been buried a long time, no need to drag it up and beat it. Clint is a sweetie and a family man now. One of his closest friends these days, is a black Baptist minister... I-I mean, one of his close associates at least." Hannah stammered, surprised at what she was hearing and saying.

Click She was answered by a dialtone.

The phrase, "only $5000." struck her as odd.

"If they know this much, I wonder if whoever this is knows I got my life savings under my seat?" she wondered. She floored the accelerator. This first investigation could be over before she started it and Tay hadn't given her a lot of time to get to the swap.

40

NOVELLA: SHADOW OF A DOUBT #20: THE TEJAS CONNECTION

"Watch your back little Tejas. Your boy Stevie tried to cut a side deal with us. His terms were a little better for me than our current arrangement, but I made it clear that for now the only way Los Zetas supplies T-Down is if you or Kayne are running it. We run a tight organization and expect the same from you. You have some hungry lieutenants who want to come up. One of them might make a move on you before Kayne gets back." Raul

Dias said looking slightly irritated at Tay through her laptop monitor.

She popped up out of her seat to respond. This was the last person on earth that she would accept advice from. Tay leaned forward and looked squarely into her laptop camera with her dark eyes narrowed to slits and exclaimed:

"Little?! What? You think I can't handle this shit on my own? I've been running things for almost a year and we still making bank, and you still making bank. I know Stevie wants my spot. That's why I clown his dumb-ass every chance I get! Its kind of sweet you think I don't know I'm choking the leashes on a pack of pits. I like 'em hungry!" she said smacking her desk repeatedly for emphasis, "If T-Down was a bunch of slack punks we would gotten rolled off the block a long time ago. I got this. He'll get his after I'm done with him if necessary." she said holding up a brass-knuckle knife in one hand and a small semi-automatic in her other, then she suppressed a smug snicker.

"I'm trying to help you. You can't lead acting unstable. Stop rolling your eyes and neck-popping at me when you're talking to me, or I swear to God I'll come after you myself." Raul said rising at his monitor and looking very much like he wanted to strangle Tay through the screen.

"Help me? Raul please! Yeah, right now you really look like you want to help me. You never helped Mami Eva when she was hiding from that lunatic that brought her over here." Tay retorted with hands on her hips.

"Nobody made Eva go over there. I told her that quack never planned to give her immigration papers, and his promised minor experimental requirements were too good to be true. I told her she could stay with me, but she always chased Gringo money. She said my place looked like a shack in somebody's backyard in the U.S. She was disrespectful and hard-headed just like you! Once her mind was made up to go, there was nothing I could do. She left with that nut who locked her up and knocked her up in his lab with a test-tube baby or something." Raul said pounding his desk with his fist in exasperation at the memory.

"You could've sent some money or something dammit! You could've told me you existed you piece of shit! So now you want to help me? It couldn't have been too hard to find a chica named Tejas. Hmph!" Tay said standing and facing away from the computer screen.

"I hoped that Eva would come back to me if she was broke. When she died, I couldn't find you. She was undocumented and I was nothing back then Bebe. I had told her before she died, that I would make it in Mexico, then come for you. I joined the Mexican army and was a good soldier. Real good. They sent me to the School of the Americas at Fort Benning, Georgia for elite Central American forces training to fight Escobar's cartel. I was still broke until they took out Escobar. Some of us fellas figured out we were in the wrong side of the drug war. We started making the real money when we took over the supply routes and started running the coca ourselves. I couldn't stay too close because if people knew you were mine they would kidnap you for ransom or kill you to get at me, no matter where you were. Plus, why in the hell would I want to help your mama who didn't want me when I was broke, even if she was mother of my kid? You wouldn't go for no shit like that!" the short dark-eyed man fumed, gesticulating wildly.

"That shit was between you two! What about me? Both of you trying to prove something to each other! You trying to prove you could make it in Mexico and her trying to prove she could make it in America! Well congratu-fuckin-lat-ions! You were right, but I've been through hell in the process! I'd have rather took my chances in Mexico than bouncing from foster home to foster home. It was fucked up in ways you can't imagine!" Tay yelled, whipping around and knocking a bunch of stuff off of her desk with a sweep of her hand in front of the camera.

"Sit down! Look at me! Listen here! I will cut you off! I don't give a shit you're my daughter! You're my kid by a whore okay? Don't think you're hot shit! I got her pregnant with you on purpose to make her quit hooking! She still left me for that godless country of yours. She claimed she wasn't sure I was the father and didn't even give you my name. Did it just to piss me off! I have killed for less disrespect than this, okay? It's ABOUT RESPECT! I come to you as a friend. It's too late to play Papi. I warn you to watch your back and you give me shit?! Our relation-ship is strictly business, but I give you a better deal than anybody else and it's the only reason T-Down undercuts everybody dealing weight there. That's my way of making up. Kayne thinks he negotiated this deal with me. BULLSHIT. I did it to make you rich after I found out where you were. Now apologize or I swear to God I'll forget I know you and you'll pay what everybody else pays! Better yet I can cut your supply off like a spigot! Raul bellowed in a spasmodic vein-bulging rage. AND CALL ME SIR! I can't stand the way you talk to me!" he yelled, gripping the desk.

"I'm sooo sahh-wwy Papi. Did I hut yo wittle feelwings?" Tay asked with mock innocence. Then she gave her father a sarcastically exaggerated repentant look. She smiled at the monitor and clicked it off. She knew it would drive him nuts.

41

NOVELLA: SHADOW OF A DOUBT #21: Interview Inferno

"Governor Jackson, is there any truth to candidate Clint Webber's allegations that the notorious Kayne Johnson is actually your brother?"

"That's news to me. Don't be ridiculous."

"Did your family ties influence your decision to pardon that drug-dealing murderer?"

"Are you implying that all black men look alike? That is all Kayne Johnson and I have in common. My brother went missing when I was a teen. I do not know his whereabouts. My family and I felt that he died long ago. It is a painful subject. Do you have the common sense or the decency, to move on?"

"Is your mother's drug abuse and alcoholism during your childhood the reason you keep pouring so much of your state's money into substance abuse treatment for addicts?"

"I don't see how things of such a personal nature are relevant to my candidacy for Senate. Try a little objective journalism for a change. I know THE LEXINGTON POST leans conservative, but you don't have to be your hometown Golden Boy's smear-monger. Come on. Be reasonable. This is unproductive. Let's start over again. Okay?"

"Is your father a mad scientist?"

"WHAT THE FUH…*ahem* How dare you characterize a deceased military veteran, exemplary Dad, and selfless medical researcher that way."

"Do you know what kind of projects he is working on right now?"

"What part of DECEASED do you not understand? You are really asking some off-the-wall questions. Is this a serious interview or some kind of sick joke?"

"Are you stone-walling me Governor, or are you really unaware of the evidence supporting these allegations that have just been made public?"

"Say what?"

"That sounded genuine."

"I just don't understand where such a load of B.S. is coming from. MY WHOLE FAMILY IS DEAD!"

"Oh my gawd...ummm...you REALLY don't know, do you? WOW. I have this information from a very reliable source. I hate to be the one to tell you this, umm sir. We are going to run this story and I am just trying to get your responses to the stuff that is floating around out there. I'm giving you a chance to defend yourself."

"It better be one HELL of a reliable source, or I swear to God I bring every force this state has to bear against this damned redneck fish-wrap! When is the last time this old decrepit pile of rubble had a building code inspection huh? I wonder if the Fire Marshal would approve of how you store your inks, paper, and flammable solvents? How are you disposing of your chemicals? HMMM…yeah! I'm sure an environmental inspector would like to know. I will shut you down! You're pathetic! Nobody reads the damned paper anymore anyway. When are you bunch of sister-kissers going get on the internet? You backwoods broke-ass conservatives never cease to amaze me! YOU ARE BROKE. HELLO. IT IS NOT IN YOUR INTEREST TO VOTE CONSERVATIVE UNTIL YOU ARE RICH!"

"Ohhhh sir…I'd say it's a reliable source. I mean, he WOULD KNOW. Kayne Johnson is saying that he is your brother, Ken Jackson III. Pending DNA results, he will be released forthwith because of mistaken identity."

cough——-"Please tell me you are making this up."—-*cough*

"Just give me a straight answer Governor. Do you confirm or deny these allegations?"

gasp—-"I won't even dignify this crap with a response. This interview is over. No more questions."—-*choke*

"You don't have a very good poker face Governor."

"I've never needed one. Have a nice day crap-spreader."

"See you on page one, Governor."

42

NOVELLA: SHADOW OF A DOUBT #22: FLASHPOINT

"WHAT THE HELL JUST HAPPENED?! HOW COULD YOU?!" Abe snarled, snatching up Doc Siskel by the lapels of his blazer and holding him eye-to-eye, close enough for his spittle to fleck the old man's face.

"I-I don't know. Let me explain! We tried to protect you. Tried-try-tried to insulate you from the family skeletons with deniability—you—you don't under-understand! Po-political liabilities Abe! Dr. Ken did it for your own good!" Siskel stammered. The sad-eyed old doctor sagged in Abe's grasp as if the wind had gone out of him with a pleading look on his liver-spotted face. His toes barely touched the ground. He was shaking.

It was at this moment that Doc noticed that Abe was a chubbier, and lighter-skinned version of his felonious brother. He could've been an intimidating goon. Doc was faced with the snorting beast that lurked suppressed beneath the politician's polished facade. It was the first time that he considered the fact Abe could have been as thuggish as Kayne if he had chosen that life.

"Is Dad ALIVE?! YEARS! YEARS! What else do I NOT KNOW? You son-of-a-bitch! YOU KNEW! I know you've been talking to Kayne. DID YOU KNOW HE WAS GOING TO TELL EVERYTHING? Tell me you didn't withhold all this from me! I thought you were a FAMILY friend. How could YOU?! What else do you know? You are slime! Goddammit! You THINK you KNOW somebody! I'm scared of what I will do to you if you don't get the FUCK outta here right now!" Abe said, with bulging bloodshot

eyes. He was so mad that he was crying without
knowing it.

He pushed his father's minion away in disgust,
and punched a hole into the sheetrock wall by his
head and strode off and slammed the door to his
office. Doc slumped against the wall with a sigh
of relief that the bones in his hollow face had not
been pulverized.

The irate Governor had just been blindsided in
an interview with a hostile newspaper by his
brother's betrayal. Now the scandal of the Governor's staying the execution of a death-row
inmate who had just revealed himself to be Abe's
long-lost brother, was blaring from every media
outlet.

Other family skeletons had fallen out the
closet in a loudly clattering heap as well. His
mother's overdose and mental illness. A father
making human clones for the military had the
religious right in a smiting mood. Abominable
creations that were the stuff of people's nightmares didn't help.

TV images of the alleged murderer and
kingpin, who had called himself Kayne Johnson
being released from prison caused an uproar.

KJIII had laughed hysterically at the gathered media, gave his middle finger to the cameras and yelled "It wasn't me!" Then he had embraced a waiting hot Latina who held a bottle of wine. They had hopped into a sinister-looking old Hummer and sped off.

Abe Jackson's little-known, small-town rival for the U.S. Senate seat suddenly took a commanding lead in the polls. Clint Webber's campaign was beating Abe Jackson over the head with the Kayne connection. Webber spoke little of what he would do if elected, he just slung mud happily, and watched the heavily-favored Governor's poll numbers take a nose-dive. The whole state was outraged. Calls for impeachment were a gurgling chorus. Some of the country folk promised vigilante justice.

The infuriated Jackson had left the interview and kicked an office chair down the hall, scattering aides and staff to their hidey-holes. Then he seized a small table upon which a sign-in ledger usually rested, and threw it into his senior campaign advisor's office with a crash, sending papers, pens, and clips flying. Abe had intended to stalk his press secretary, but had caught the unfortunate Doc Siskel signing-in for a damage-control visit on an errand for Jackson's Machiavellian father.

His staff and most of the reserved and well-dressed political aides and handlers were scratching their heads and looking at each other nervously until the one-man storm abated. Some cowered in cubicles and offices and popped up occasionally to look around like prairie-dogs. They had never seen such a violent outburst in their sheltered world of the best and brightest. The confusion over whether to call security on the Governor seemed to be main source of bewilderment.

The stained walnut door to the Governor's office flung open and Abe stormed out and took the still stunned Doc Siskel by the elbow. He leaned close to his father's confidant and began escorting him roughly towards the exit to the parking lot.

"Let's go old man! Where is dear old Dad?! We're going for a ride! Let's get this shit straightened out right now. You get to be my GPS! Let's take your car. You get to be the wheel-man!" Abe growled.

Doc Siskel resigned himself to the situation and gained a bit of confidence and composure.

"You KNOW this is assault and battery don't you Governor?" he said forcing a chattering grin as Abe pushed him into the driver's seat of his Saab cabriolet and slammed his car-door shut. Then Abe rushed to clamber into the other side of the car.

"Tell me something I don't know. I'm a fucking lawyer. I'm not planning anything so we can up it to man-slaughter if you don't take me straight to my old man's hideout! Now DRIVE!"

A gunshot rang out and shattered the glass in the passenger window. A second shot cracked the air, and Abe slumped over into Siskel's blood-flecked lap with a prolonged sigh.

43

NOVELLA: SHADOW OF A DOUBT #23: EXTREME MEASURES

"They are trying to kill me Doc! Get us outta here!" Abe gasped, pushing himself up with his left elbow on the center console, and clutching his chest with his other hand, while trying to right himself in the passenger seat as Siskel zoomed towards the hospital. Blood bubbled from between his fingers on his chest. Some glass was stuck in his face.

"Don't talk sonny! Where are you hit?" Siskel asked, trying to determine where Abe bled from and drive at break-neck speed at once.

"I—I don't know where am I hit? Oh God my chest! God…can't breathe Doc, am I —am I gonna die? Shit…uhgghh."

"Stop talking! You won't die! Don't quit on me! Hold on! We're almost there! I think you got a sucking chest wound…didn't get your heart or we wouldn't be talking right now. Don't be scared! I think you'll be okay…just don't talk… save your air my boy. I'm gonna move heaven and hell to get us there in time! Trust me…I'm a doctor…remember!" Doc yelled, shifting quickly through the gears and jerking the steering wheel hard left.

SCREEEEEEEEEEEEEEEEEEEEEEEEE!!!— the tires squealed.

"You're driving like a medical examiner Doc… I need somebody to keep me alive not check me out once I'm dead…you're gonna kill us driving like this!" *gasp*

The Saab's turbo screamed and rubber squealed as the white-knuckled Siskel careened the car around corners and zoomed in and out of traffic and through city streets. Governor Jackson had picked the right wheel-man after all. The little old man could drive his ass off.

Hannah Webber, the rival Senate campaign's private investigator, alone had staked out the rear of the building to track the Governor's movements. Her former cop instinct had served her well, with the exception that she had left her gun in her car a block away. She saw the shooter. It was near dusk and she thought her eyes were playing tricks on her.

"I ain't even drink no white lightning today. Oh Lawd. Clint ain't gonna believe this!" she murmured in quiet disbelief, and adjusted her binoculars.

A black-clad figure in special ops gear, small in stature, had emerged from the surrounding tree canopy and alit as silently as a mosquito behind a hedge approximately 75 meters away from Doc's car shortly before firing two shots. The first had shattered the glass. The second had struck the Governor. The shooter arrived within 30 seconds of Doc and the Governor exiting the building. It had to have been set-up.

Hannah was shocked by the shooter's method of transportation. What could only be described as a bi-copter uniform device (two small helicopter blades with individual engines, spun above each shoulder of the would-be assassin who wore a harness attached to the branching flight frame contraption). It moved so swiftly and silently that it could almost be described as flitting instead of flying. Once the mark was hit, the dark figure spoke briefly on a wireless helmet mike, while it flitted back into the darkness below the tree-line.

The media that had been waiting to ambush the Governor out in front of his offices had charged around back at the sound of the gunshots. A news helicopter provided live video of the Governor's race against time and arrival at the hospital. All the scandalous stories they came to cover suddenly took a back-burner to the assassination attempt. Who did it? Why? Where were they? Would anyone claim responsibility? Was race a motive? The media machine began churning in earnest. Reporters were everywhere. Breaking news on the event hit every media outlet.

No one paid attention to an old dark blue 1986 Buick Park Avenue that slowly wound its way toward the hospital from the other direction. It had a little a security escort of four black-clad female troopers who were armed to the teeth and riding motorcycles.

Dr. Ken Jackson Jr. talked on his wireless to a procurement operative clone that had carried out a special assignment. He had wanted to see how easily she could be reprogrammed for a different kind of mission. He wanted his new team of Peregrine-class clones to be able to subcontract for various military operations. It was his surplus inventory solution. Peregrines were usually used for kidnapping or material retrievals. Dr. Ken had made a point of limiting their level of intelligence to that necessary for them to complete their missions. He didn't want them thinking for themselves because then they might begin to consider themselves people.

"Target hit sir. Right upper thoracic. Should be non-fatal with immediate medical care. I'm surprised you didn't request a tranquilizer round." Peregrine One intoned.

"This is more dramatic. People might suspect something if a tranquilizer round was used. No-no...now this...is something they can believe... haha...and come up with someone to blame... like a lone gun nut Clint Webber supporter...

hopefully. My purpose is served. Excellent execution." Dr. Jackson observed.

"Thank you sir. Execution? I hit right-chest not left-chest sir." Peregrine One droned.

"I guess I need to explain the nuances of the English language to you again Peregrine one. You have passed this evaluation in the best manner possible. Return to base. Extra oxygen and an MRE instead of intravenous for you tonight." Dr. Ken commended.

"Thank you sir. Returning to base. Out." was the monotone response.

Dr. Ken smiled in satisfaction and continued driving fifteen miles below the speed limit. He hadn't drove in many years. It was sort of fun. He always enjoyed a great counter-move in his chess games. He felt he had just made one.

"Extreme betrayals require extreme counter-measures. These vultures who wanted to pick his bones this afternoon will be covering a candle-light vigil for him tonight. They are fickle creatures. I AM NOT. Kayne's betrayal can't stop our rise. My dear, are you enjoying the ride? I want you to meet someone. You may recognize him. I hope you do. He will be thrilled to see you I'm sure, maybe not so much. We are going to have a family reunion of sorts." he said gently patting his wife, Bette on the hand.

She looked at him and smiled absently. Bette often feigned recognition, though most of the time she seemed to have no idea what her husband was talking about. She returned to gazing in child-like wonder out her car-window at all the sights and sounds of the city as they passed through.

44

NOVELLA: SHADOW OF A DOUBT #24: CONCIOUS

Dr. Ken Jackson Jr. waited patiently with his wife, Bette, for his son, Governor Abe Jackson to emerge from surgery. He had been alerted that the gunshot victim was in critical condition but would soon be moved from surgery to this room to recover. A close family friend, Doc Siskel, paced the room, riddled with guilt for his performance in a macabre play in the house Jackson built.

Dr. Ken smiled to himself. This world was peopled with so many trusting souls. He had masterminded his son's shooting, but he was welcomed by the hospital and the public by pretending that he only emerged from his shadowy black ops lair out of concern for his son.

Who would've thought that the distinguished old scientist, so tenderly stroking his wife's hand, was willing to spill his son's blood to accomplish his goals.

The four heavily-armed guards close to the couple should have drawn more suspicion, but someone had taken a shot at his son. Surely, it was understandable why the rumored clone-lord had a security detail. Most of the general public thought that the clones were in the near future, but a close inspection of Dr. Ken's guards would've revealed that fully functioning military operative clones were already in production. They looked like younger versions of his wife.

All was going according to Dr. Ken's plan. Governor Abe's support had rallied in the Senate race polls. The prodigal son, KJIII aka Kayne, was free. That was fine as long as he was too far away to cause trouble. The clones education for military variations was going amazingly well. They were faster learners than he had imagined.

Bette's recovery was near total. Dr. Ken and his initial investor and friend, Doc Siskel were finally set to rake in huge military profits after years of researching clones with little funding, and working underground.

Dr. Ken always planned ahead. The problem was he didn't look behind him often enough. He barely detected Bette giving a slight nod to one of the Talon-class security escort clones. Then he felt a blade almost too sharp to cause pain flick past the right-side of his collar, followed by a gush of warm metallic-scented ooze. As his last thoughts faded, he diagnosed himself quickly. His external jugular had been severed and he was quickly bleeding out. He watched dully losing consciousness as Doc Siskel suffered a similar surgically precise strike, and the two clones that weren't wielding knives began bundling him up into a big black plastic garbage bag.

"You conniving snakes shot my baby boy. What kind of Mom would I be if I let that shit go? Take out this trash my dears." Bette scolded. Then she smiled triumphantly.

The Talons discreetly pushed the two garbage bags into waiting hospital laundry carts, covered them with laundry. Then they quickly changed into nurse aide unis and exited with their cargo two by two.

Dr. Ken had not been aware of a secret development that his creations had kept among themselves. He had tried to limit their intelligence by limiting their education to the necessary and their brains to a bare functional minimum of oxygen supply. He had limited their food to intravenous supplies and gave military food rations only as rewards. He had shipped the male clones out as fast as they reached adolescence to waiting military governments, in part to prevent romantic notions between the sexes of his clones. Control every human impulse. That had been his mantra.

Dr. Ken had made clones and expected them not to be people. They resented that. They feigned ignorance, but they shared a collective will. They all had one genetic mother: Bette. They inherited her animosity to Dr. Ken and when one learned something, they secretly taught the rest of their sisters. An unintended consequence of their cloning was that they became a harmonious female unit. This had sped up when the good doctor had delegated the teaching to trusted clones. Soon he had a hive on hands and had no clue he was holding it.

Bette's awakening had been the arrival of the queen bee to the waiting hive. She had planned an attack to wipe the would-be clone-master from the face of the earth. She wanted to set her girls free. Sure, it would be kind of weird, but they could live the life that she had given up for that megalomaniac man of hers.

"When in the presence of a know-it-all, play dumb!" had been their collective mantra, that she had authored. It had worked, because the brilliant scientist had never saw them coming.

Bette thought about Kayne. He had always been trouble. Hell, he had tried to come out of her side when she had given birth to him, until he got himself turned around. She wondered if he would've ended up the way he was if Dr.Ken had been offed long ago. She shook her head with a sigh. Then she prepared to greet her wounded and favored son, Abe Jackson, alone.

She ran over to Abe and squeezed his hand when he was wheeled in on a gurney. His eyes blinked open and watered upon seeing her.

45

LIVING LIFE IN PAST TENSE

The voices in my head,

A wailing choir chants,
I would've, I could've, I should've, I can't,
Grips slipped on victories,
Siren songs rant,
I would've, I could've, I should've, I can't,
Nothing's permanent,
Crushed in an instant,
I would've, I could've, I should've, I can't,
Life's going on,
Spoken of as distant,
I would've, I could've, I should've, I can't,
So many missed chances,

Doors slammed on opportunities,
Cursed with a rebel's heart,
And a mind bordering on lunacy,
Can't move forward,
Best days are behind me,
Try to drink away the pain,
Does nothing but remind me,
Bartender knows my name,
Favorite draft is poured,
Before I sit at the bar,
After I enter the door,
After beer after beer,
Followed by shot after shot,
They don't want me to drive,
Why do they have parking lots?
Cops waiting outside,
Marked my tires with chalk,
Know how long I've been inside,
Am I supposed to walk?
Catch me if you can,
Put the petal to the floor,
Put the music on blast,
Psych myself up for—
The big finish,
Where metal meets my mind,

Tasted sweet flesh of life,
Embittered with the rind,
Roulette spin the chambers,
Pull, pray, and pant,
I would've, I could've, I should've, I can't.

46

MISS AFRICAN AMERICAN PIE

Golden brown peach cobbler,

Miss african-american pie,

Lord I should've tasted,

When she offered me a try,

Any way you slice it,

I'd have to say I missed out,

But I choose to be happy,

My head's often in the clouds,

Running with a kite-string,

On which I had no hold,

She floated away at a concert,

To the stage for a singer of soul,

Man, I couldn't help smiling,

As I watched her ascent,

Out of sight the rest of the night,

Couldn't tell where my plaything went,

And now so many years later,

I guess I gotta confess,

A nostalgic wish for such a dish,

Answer unequivocal--YES!

She's hanging with luminaries,

I stargaze from the ground,

Just a fleeting singularity,

In her memory's lost & found,

I see her in the night sky,

Twinkling eyes of brown,

Think of letting her go at that show,

I'm glad I didn't keep her down.